WANDERVILLE

Escape to the World's Fair

WENDY McCLURE

WANDERVILLE

Escape to the World's Fair

razor
bill

An Imprint of Penguin Group (USA)

Penguin.com
Razorbill, an Imprint of Penguin Random House

ISBN: 978-1-59514-820-9

Printed in the United States of America

1 3 5 7 9 10 8 6 4 2

Interior design by Eric Ford

1
A RUN-IN WITH FATE

*D*own, Jack thought as he pulled the handle. *Down.* He pulled again. *Down.*

The great iron arm creaked, and every so often the wheels would scrape as they slid along the tracks. Sometimes the scraping noise was so sharp Jack could hear it with his teeth. But it meant that they were making the handcar go as fast as it could—enough speed for a breeze that turned Frances's hair wild and nearly blew Alexander's cap away—and that was worth it. Even if all five of them wound up bone tired by nightfall again, at least they were going somewhere, right?

As far as Jack could tell, they were in Missouri still—the rusty stretch of railroad track they were on went past quiet cornfields and meadows. Twice they'd seen people—once, when they went by a farmhouse yard where a woman tended a clothesline, and then later, when they passed a man with a horse and plow. Frances's little brother, Harold, had called out hello to them and waved, but the woman had only stared back in amazement and the man had scratched his head. Jack figured it had been years and years since a train had traveled on these tracks, much less a handcar with five kids on board.

The fewer folks they saw, though, the better. They had a long way to travel, after all. Jack had been thinking about it all morning, and he was sure the others were, too. *California!* He couldn't believe they were on their way. But then he'd watch the big iron arm on the handcar go up and down like a seesaw and wonder how many times he'd have to pump those handles before they got to California.

Down. Jack pulled again and shifted his weight on his aching feet. Today he was riding backward. When they'd first found the handcar two days ago, Jack and Frances had taken the side that faced forward, while Alexander and Eli had been on the other side. Sometimes they all switched places, and while it hadn't taken Jack long to get used to the motion of riding that way, he hated that the only thing he could see were the trees and fields behind their vehicle, slipping away into the distance.

"What's . . . ahead?" he managed to ask between deep breaths. "What . . . can . . . you see?"

Eli, who, along with Alexander, had the proper view, shook his head. "Nothin'," he puffed as he pulled down the handles on his end. "Same old . . . thing . . . Fields and stuff."

Harold piped up. "That ain't nothing!" He rode in the middle and held on to their supplies since he was seven and too young to work the handles on the handcar. "I see a big tree, and a barn way over there. . . ."

"*Isn't*," Frances corrected him. She was pulling right next to Jack, but she still had to be the big sister. "Not . . . *ain't*."

Jack had a feeling it was going to be another long day. Yesterday they'd kept the handcar going well after dusk, until they were so exhausted they could barely speak. They'd stumbled off the tracks and fell onto the nearest bit of grass they could find. Jack's arms had felt sore to the bones, Frances complained of blisters, and Eli had declared that working the handcar was tougher than plowing.

"Just wait," Alexander had said last night,

while they all stretched out in the prickly prairie grass trying to find comfortable spots for sleeping. "Next thing you know, we'll be eating oranges out west. . . ."

His had voice trailed off. Nobody else had spoken; they hadn't had the energy to reply.

Jack was glad the five of them were on their own now, and not back at Reverend Carey's farm. Or, worse, still on an orphan train or breaking their backs at the ranch in Kansas. They were free, which meant that they *had* to be better off now.

That's what he kept telling himself, at least. *We're lucky.* He'd say it in his head all day long today if he had to. In between pulling the handle, that is. *Down . . . down.* He knew there were other kids who weren't so lucky.

An hour or so passed, and then another rusty shriek from the handcar wheels snapped Jack out of his thoughts. The awful sound grew louder, and Jack could feel himself cringing.

"Ow!" Harold cried, his voice barely carrying above the noise. *"Ow!"*

"What?" Frances called back to her brother. "What is it?"

Harold's eyes were wide as he looked past Jack

and Frances to the tracks ahead. And suddenly Jack realized what Harold was saying. Not *ow* but *look out!*

"We have to stop—" Alexander began. He and Eli could see whatever was ahead too, and they had quit working the handle.

"We have to *brake!*" Eli cut in. "Where's the brake?"

"Here!" Frances reached for it, an iron lever near her feet. She yanked on it with both hands.

The handcar screeched and slowed just enough for Jack to turn around and see the tracks ahead.

Or rather, what was *left* of the tracks.

Where's the bridge? Frances's mouth went dry when she turned and spotted the creek ahead. Where there should have been a bridge, the tracks instead ended in two bent pieces that reached over the high bluff of the creek bank.

"We have to get off this thing!" Jack cried.

The handcar was still going plenty fast, its brake noise shrill and awful. The bank was just a few yards away and coming closer. Frances reached across to grab Harold's sleeve, getting ready to pull him along into a well-timed jump—

But with a bump and a *BANG!*, the handcar

slammed to a sudden stop. Frances lost her footing and toppled off one side, dragging Harold with her.

"Ooof!" She hit the ground hard on her backside.

Alexander stumbled over and offered her a hand. "You all right?"

Frances nodded and got up. She looked around: Her brother had managed to land on his feet, though he'd dropped the floursack full of supplies. Jack and Eli had gone off the other side of the handcar, and they were slowly pulling themselves off the ground.

"What just happened?" she murmured.

"It's broken!" Harold cried, pointing over to where the handcar stood tilted to one side like a collapsed table. "The wheels came off the track!"

"Looks like it derailed," Alexander said. He showed Frances and the others a spot along the tracks where two lengths of rail had come apart.

Frances looked over by the creek where the tracks abruptly ended. The bridge must have fallen long ago, and the rails on the bank had buckled. She was glad that the handcar hadn't just pitched them all straight into the rocky creek bed, but now that it had gone off the rails it was useless. She watched as Jack kicked the handcar wheels, his jaw set. He reached up and yanked the big iron arm, which made a feeble creak.

"Forget it," Eli said to Jack. "That thing isn't going anywhere."

Frances knew Eli was right. Even if they could fix it, there was no way they could haul it across the creek to where the tracks continued. She stepped closer to the wreck and sighed when she saw the snapped cables and a big splintery crack down one side of the platform.

"That was our treasure," she said softly.

I'm sorry, Ned Handsome, she thought to herself. Ned was a hobo they'd met while riding the rails out of Kansas. Before they'd parted ways, he'd given them a mysterious set of directions leading to a "treasure" he'd stashed away. For weeks Frances had puzzled over the clues and dreamed of finding it.

And she had; she'd found the handcar. Over the past two days they'd used it to travel more than sixty miles all by themselves. It had seemed like there'd be no stopping them. *Until now.*

Frances had to bite her lip to keep back the tears. She glanced up to see Alexander looking over solemnly, as if to say he was sorry too. It helped to know that he understood.

Harold came over to her side and squeezed her hand. "Don't be sad, Frannie. Nobody got hurt too bad."

She squeezed his hand back. "You're right. We're lucky." She was glad for the reminder. It could have been much worse. But Harold had nothing more than a couple of dirty scuffs on his knickers, Frances and Alexander had just a few scrapes and bruises, and Eli had a skinned knee that he was washing in the creek. As for Jack, he seemed unhurt, but his shoulders slumped and he rubbed his eyes like he had a terrible headache.

"What do we do now?" Jack asked, looking around at all of them. "How are we ever going to get to California?"

Nobody answered for a moment. But Frances turned to look at Alexander. She had a feeling he'd have something to say.

"That's a good question, Jack," he said. "But for now, we start by walking."

2
SECOND THOUGHTS ON THE ROAD

"*Walking?*" Jack repeated. "You mean, just keep following these tracks? On foot?"

The five of them had picked up the supplies that had scattered in the crash and were now trudging down the bank to the edge of the creek. Alexander led the way, carrying the water jar.

"Sure," Alexander said as he knelt to refill the jar in the creek. "Remember what Ned said about these rails? This is supposed to be a back road that goes halfway to Oklahoma."

"We might as well keep going," Frances added.

"Sure," Jack replied, though *sure* was the last thing he felt right now.

When he reached the creek he bent down and plunged his hands into the stream. They'd been smarting like crazy ever since he'd used them to break his fall in the crash—he'd already had a blister on one palm from working the handcar pump handles. For a few moments he tried to soothe his hands in the cool water, feeling the chill of the stream creep up his tired arms.

"You coming?" Eli called.

Jack looked up to see that the other four were making their way over the creek, using stepping-stones to cross the water. Alexander was already starting to climb up the opposite bank. Jack sighed and got up to follow his friends.

Soon they were all walking alongside the rail line, a single set of tracks that ran past a muddy meadow and stretched on as far as they could see.

"How far is halfway to Oklahoma?" Harold asked, looking up at his sister.

"Shush, Harold," Frances replied. "We need to concentrate on where we're going."

After that, nobody else said anything for a while. It was hot, and sometimes, when they passed swaths of taller grass, gnats and mosquitoes would drift around them, stinging their arms.

Jack was glad that the walk was easy, at least. You didn't even have to hold your head up as long as you kept your eyes on the tracks. He wasn't in the mood to do anything besides stare at his feet. But the less he had to think about where he was going, the more he thought about everything else. About everyone . . .

"What's with you, Jack?" Frances kept looking over her shoulder at him as she walked, her face full of concern.

"Yeah, what's wrong?" Eli asked.

"Nothing," Jack said. He didn't want to talk about what was on his mind. But his steps grew slower and slower.

A few yards up ahead, Alexander stopped and turned. "Don't you want to keep going?" he asked Jack.

Harold came over and peered up at him. "We're going to find Wanderville again, Jack," he said, his voice hopeful. "I know we are."

Wanderville—the town they'd created themselves. First they'd built it in the woods in Kansas, where they'd escaped from the orphan trains and the Pratcherds' work ranch. Then, when they'd found a shelter for a while at Reverend Carey's farm in Missouri, Wanderville was behind the barn.

Wanderville could be anywhere, they'd decided,

but it wasn't everywhere. It had to be a place where
they felt truly safe. A place where other kids could
come live, too. *All kids in need of freedom,* Alexander
had said. And they were hoping that in California
they could build Wanderville in a permanent spot.

Only it didn't seem possible now. Not to Jack.
Not at all.

He clenched his blistered hand to try to keep
it from stinging. He looked down at Harold, and
then over at Eli and Alexander and Frances, their
shoes and stockings caked with mud. *Walking,* their
only possessions the grimy clothes on their backs, a
few meager provisions stowed in a flour sack, and a
cracked jar of creek water.

"I don't know about Wanderville," Jack found
himself saying suddenly. "Or California." He
couldn't stop the words from rushing out, all his
awful thoughts. "Maybe we won't get there. Maybe
it's just hopeless."

Harold's face fell and he stepped away from Jack.

Alexander was incredulous. "How can you say
that? *Why?*"

Jack took a deep breath and picked up his pace.
"All we want is a better life, but things just keep getting worse for us." He paused to wipe some extra

mud off his shoe, then continued. "We keep trying to save other kids. But—but it's no use. Because we . . ."

He was saying *we*, but deep down he felt like it was really *his* job to save other kids. He'd wanted to rescue all the kids on the orphan trains and all the kids who'd been sent to work at the Pratcherds'. And before that, back in New York, he'd wanted to save Daniel from the fire at the factory. His older brother, Daniel . . .

"We keep losing them," he said softly.

Jack was striding even faster now, kicking at the gravel between the railroad ties. The other four hurried to keep up with him.

"But Jack," Frances began, "we *did* save other kids. We rescued six kids from the Pratcherds. . . ."

He shook his head. "And where are they now? Quentin and Lorenzo ran off to join some hoboes. Then the rest of them—we lost them, too."

It still stung to think about how much bigger their group had been. When they'd first stayed at the Careys' farm there had been eight of them. But Sarah, Anka, Nicky, and George had decided they'd rather live in Reverend Carey's big house than in Wanderville.

"Look, we're better off without them," Alexander said, a bit defensively.

"Are we?" Jack asked. "Look at us, limping along in the middle of nowhere. We can't even save ourselves!"

Nobody said anything for a moment; they all just kept putting one foot in front of the other.

It was Eli who finally broke the silence. "Well, you saved *me*," he said.

Eli had lived in one of the shanties in back of the Careys' place. His father was a sharecropper who drank too much and had a terrible temper that he'd take out on Eli sometimes. So when Jack, Alexander, Frances, and Harold had left the farm, Eli had joined them.

Jack relaxed enough to manage a half smile. "Glad you're here, Eli," he said.

"Come on," Frances insisted. "It's not completely hopeless, is it? How do you think *I* felt when we crashed Ned's treasure? But you don't see *me* giving up, do you?"

Jack thought she had a point. But things still felt pretty dismal.

Alexander was walking right alongside Jack now. "We've just got to keep going. Our luck will change, Jack, I know it will. We'll find other ways to travel.

There will be other kids we can bring to Wanderville. Other people who will need our help."

"Like that man over there," Harold said, matter-of-factly.

"What?" Frances said. "*What* man?"

"In the motorcar." Harold pointed across the meadow.

There, in the distance, was a big green-and-black touring car. There was no road in sight, yet oddly the car sat in the middle of a field, its engine silent, its two front wheels sunk into mud.

The five children stopped short. "What is an *automobile* doing out *here*?" Alexander wondered aloud.

"It's stuck!" Harold declared. "And the man driving it is looking for help."

Jack squinted at the far-off figure in the car. Harold was right: The man was standing up in the front seat, looking all around. The man turned in their direction and stopped, as if he could see them.

Uh-oh, Jack thought. The last thing they needed right now was another grown-up asking them questions.

"Harold, what are you *doing*?" Frances exclaimed.

Jack turned to see that Harold was waving his arms to get the man's attention. The man waved back.

"Look, we can't just go talking to strangers," Alexander warned.

But Harold had already climbed over the tracks and was running through the meadow, heading straight for the man in the motorcar.

3
THE MOTORCAR IN THE MUD

"That's my sister," Harold was saying to the man by the time Frances reached her brother's side. She and the others had run after Harold, but they hadn't been able to stop him from talking to the stranger, who had climbed out of the car and was using a cloth to dust off one of the fenders.

"And these are my friends," Harold continued, motioning to Jack and Alexander and Eli. "We escaped from the orphan trains, except for Eli, who—"

"*Harold!*" Frances snapped. She turned to the man. "I'm so sorry, sir, my little brother likes to make up stories and—"

The fellow held up his palm. "Say no more, mademoiselle. I mind my own business." He tipped his hat and nodded at Frances and the boys. "Name's Philander Zogby, and I humbly solicit your assistance."

"That means you need help, right?" Harold asked.

Mr. Zobgy nodded. Frances couldn't help noticing how dandyish he appeared—his cap was checkered, his suit striped, and he had a mustache that drew up into points like a bull's horns. But under his mustache she could see that he was young, not much older than eighteen or nineteen, and it was hard for her to think of him as *Mister* Zogby.

He gave one of the front tires of the car a soft kick. "As you can see, my Cleveland Tonneau has found misadventure," he explained. "I've been heading to St. Louis, on my way to the Fair, but these country roads aren't made for motoring.

"I tried to take a shortcut through this nice meadow, but it seems meadows aren't made for motoring, either."

Frances and the others bent down by the front of the car for a closer look.

The mud in the meadow wasn't too wet, but it was soft, and the motorcar's front wheels had sunk down into it, the tires forming two deep ruts.

Alexander straightened up. "I don't know, sir. That . . . Cleveland thing of yours is awfully big."

And *nice*, Frances thought. The car had brass fittings on the headlamps and shiny upholstered seats. It looked pretty out of place in the middle of a meadow. *Too* out of place, in fact.

"We can't just *drag* it out," Alexander continued.

"Of course not!" Zogby said. "But we can put something under the wheels so they don't keep digging into that mud. . . ."

Jack was nodding now. "And then we can push it from the back!" he said.

Jack seemed glad to help this Zogby fellow, Frances noticed. She looked over at the others. Alexander's face was wary—Eli's, too. Harold was busy gazing at the shiny brass edge of the car's front grille.

She didn't trust this fellow in his fancy duds and gaudy motorcar, but he sure looked like he had nickels to spare. Maybe, if they managed to get him out of this jam, he'd help them out, too.

Alexander caught her eye and shrugged. He seemed to be thinking the same thing.

"Well . . . all right," he said. "Let's get to work."

Jack and Harold were already collecting twigs and sticks to put under the motorcar, laying them across the ruts in the mud and wedging them under the tires. When they'd gathered as many sticks as they could, Zogby began to work the engine crank.

"Get ready," he called.

Alexander and Eli and Jack went to the back of the car, while Harold clambered up into the rear seat.

"What are you doing?" Frances scolded. "Get down from there!"

"Er . . . I told him he could give the orders," Zogby said with a grin as he cranked.

"*What* orders?" she said, but suddenly her voice was drowned out by the chugging engine as it sputtered to life.

"PUSH!" Harold yelled at the top of his lungs.

The three older boys pushed against the back of the car. It rocked forward a bit, then shook as the front wheels struggled to find traction.

"PUSH!" Harold called again, but the wheels still spun in place despite the boys' best efforts.

Frances looked at Zogby, who was now in the driver's seat, fiddling with some valves, and then at her friends. Jack and Eli had dug their heels into the soft ground, while Alexander locked his arms and pressed his hands. She couldn't tell if they were pushing really hard or just making a big show out of pushing. She went over and found a spot next to Alexander.

"We don't need help," he said, gasping.

"Sure you do," she said. Then she gave the car a good shove the next time Harold called *PUSH*.

They all felt a big *bump,* and then the motorcar lurched forward.

"Excellent!" Zogby shouted.

Jack and Eli whooped with triumph. Frances, meanwhile, grinned at Alexander. He smiled back, though he looked a little sheepish, too.

The car chugged a few yards over to drier ground. "Climb aboard!" Zogby called. "I'll take you back to town!"

"*What?*" Frances cried. It was one thing to help this fellow, but it was another to go off somewhere with him in that automobile. "I don't think this is such a great idea," she muttered.

"Come on," Jack whispered. "I think he's all right. And besides, we really ought to find a map soon. Maybe there'll be one in the next town."

Alexander didn't look as sure as Jack, but Eli was

already climbing up into the car, and Harold was practically bouncing with excitement.

"Can I ride in front, Frannie?" he asked.

Frances sighed. "Fine, but you'll have to sit with me."

A moment later she was perched up on the front seat with Harold and Zogby, while the three boys sat in back. She'd never been in a motorcar before—the seats were almost as high as a buggy's, and the chugging engine made everything shake like a nervous dog. It felt a little like the freight car she'd ridden to Kansas City, but the noise was different—a constant sputtering from the engine that threatened to drown out everything else. In fact, Zogby had to shout over it as he steered the car across the meadow and onto a road.

"WHICH TOWN?" he called. "WHERE ARE YOU HEADED?"

Frances turned back to look at the boys, but Jack only shrugged.

"ANIMAL, RIGHT?" Zogby shouted. "ANIMAL?"

Frances and the boys all exchanged confused looks. *What is he talking about?* But then Eli's face lit up, as if he'd just realized something. "Yes!" he shouted. "Hannibal!"

Suddenly Frances understood, too: *Hannibal.* That was a town in Missouri. She hoped it wasn't far. This Zogby fellow seemed decent enough, but she didn't know how long she could listen to him talk over the engine.

"I WAS HEADING TO ST. LOUIS MYSELF!" he shouted. "FOR THE WORLD'S FAIR! HAVE YOU HEARD?" He looked over at Frances and Harold, who shook their heads.

"THE LOUISIANA PURCHASE EXPOSITION!" he went on. "THE PAPERS SAY IT'S A MARVEL."

"A *FAIR*?" Harold yelled.

"*MORE* THAN A FAIR," Zogby shouted back. "IT'S A LAND OF PALACES! THEY BUILT A CITY NEXT TO THE CITY AND IT'S ALL GRAND PALACES! THEY'VE GOT THAT OBSERVATION WHEEL THAT'S TWO HUNDRED FEET HIGH!"

Just then a stiff breeze picked up and filled Frances's ears with wind, and then she could hear only bits and snatches of Zogby's words.

"ELECTRICAL . . . BIGGEST EVER! . . . TEN-MILLION-DOLLAR PIKE! . . . A MILE LONG!"

Frances could only shrug, though she could see that Jack and Eli were leaning forward in the backseat as if trying to catch every word. Finally Zogby pulled over by the side of the road and cut the engine so he could continue.

". . . and there's an exhibit for nearly every country in the world! And oh, the amusements! You can ride the Golden Chariot or the Fairyland Chutes. Or visit the Ostrich Farm, or the Telegraph Tower, or the Moorish Palace. I hear they've even got a horse on display that can read and write and do sums!"

Frances tried not to roll her eyes. This place sounded loony. And it couldn't be any better than Coney Island back in New York, which had electric lights everywhere and was only really fun until you got sick of the crowds and the smell of fried clams.

Harold, for his part, was nodding at everything Zogby said. "Wow," he breathed. "Can we come with you to the Fair, Mr. Zogby?"

The young man grinned. "It would be great fun to go, wouldn't it?"

"YES," Jack and Eli said in unison.

"Except we're going to *California*," Alexander said sternly. "Remember?"

Harold bounced in his seat. "'Zander! Can we go to the St. Louis Fair first, please? With Mr. Zogby?"

"*Harold!*" Frances scolded. "Mr. Zogby did *not* say he would take us to the World's Fair!" She thought Zogby should know better than to talk about the Fair like that and give a kid like Harold ideas. *Just what is he trying to do, anyway?*

Zogby nodded. "Indeed, I said nothing of the sort," he replied. "Because, as it turns out, I will not be attending after all." His fingers tapped the steering wheel as if he were thinking. "This trip has had some . . . er, complications, and I realized that it's best if I return to Chicago."

"Oh," Harold mumbled.

"Yes, it's a shame," Zogby said, staring off into the distance. "But perhaps," he said, turning in his seat to look at all of them, "*you'll* go the World's Fair. You'll go *instead* of me. Go in my place!"

4
TOO GOOD TO BE TRUE?

Jack was too stunned to say anything for a moment. Judging from the long silence, everyone else was, too.

The first person to speak was Frances.

"Oh, we're *going*, all right," she said, opening the car door on her side and jumping to the ground. "We're going to walk the rest of the way to Hannibal, thank you very much."

"Wait!" Zogby replied. "Please, I can explain . . ."

Frances shook her head. "We're not getting into some ridiculous scheme." She tugged Harold's sleeve, then Eli's. "Come on, everyone."

"*Wait!*" Jack blurted out. He hadn't planned on speaking up; it had just happened. Out of the corner of his eye he could see Alexander glaring at him, his hand on the latch of the car door. Alexander had been just about to get out.

"I mean," Jack went on, "let's hear what he has to say."

Zogby spoke up. "I can certainly elaborate further. See, I have some business at the Fair that I wish I could attend to, but . . . I can't. It's better if I don't go."

Jack wondered why, but there was something sort of strange in Zogby's eyes that made him decide it was better not to ask.

But Alexander narrowed his eyes. "Your business sounds awfully secret."

"Which is exactly why you're just the right people to go in my stead. You're kids—nobody will notice you. And you're—" Zogby seemed to search for the right words. "Well, I get the sense that you're on your own, yes?"

He looked right at Jack, who nodded *yes*.

"You look smart, the whole lot of you. I bet you've had to get through some tough times."

He's got that right, Jack thought.

"This *business* you're in," Frances said, a little sarcastically. "Is it against the law?"

"Not any—" Zogby began, then corrected himself. "Not *at all*, I mean."

ck wanted to believe him, and he was pretty sure Eli did, too. But he glanced over at Frances and Alexander, who were exchanging wary looks with each other. Clearly they didn't trust Zogby one bit.

"Look," Zogby said. "All you have to do is deliver *this* for me." He reached into his striped suit-coat jacket and pulled out an object wrapped in a silk handkerchief. He held it out as he uncovered it. At the first glimpse of something shiny they all leaned in for a closer look. Even Frances had come back to the side of the car to take a peek.

Jack saw metal—dull gold, and a glinting chain. The thing was a medallion of some kind, covered with elaborate sculpted designs. Zogby turned it over so they all could see both sides. On one side was a bird—a hawk or a falcon of some kind—with outstretched wings, and on the other, an ox with a crown on its head.

"*Whoa,*" Jack said under his breath.

The medallion was big enough to cover Zogby's palm, and there was some kind of writing all along the edge. Not writing, Jack suddenly realized—*symbols.*

Eli drew back suddenly. "What *is* that thing?" To Jack it seemed like he practically jumped.

"*What* it is isn't important," Zogby told him.

"But I promise it won't bite. You can hold it if you like." He held out the medallion to Eli, but the boy shook his head *no*.

Jack took it instead. It felt heavy in his hand. Expensive.

Frances reached out to hold it, too. "Is it stolen?"

"I promise you it is not," Zogby replied. "But it is very valuable, and my . . . my associate will give you a spectacular reward for bringing it to the Fair."

"Hmm," Frances said, weighing the medallion in her hand. Harold peered over her arm at the thing but would not touch it. Alexander kept his hands in his pockets.

It seemed to Jack that whatever the thing was, it was important. It made him think of the gold watch that his brother, Daniel, had once pointed out to him in the window at Segal's on New Chambers Street. He'd been saving his wages to buy it. "Imagine having a treasure like that in your vest," Daniel had said. "Bet it makes you really feel like you're someone."

Zogby's voice brought Jack back to the present.

"Well?" he asked. "Can I count on you all to deliver this safely to the Louisiana Purchase Exposition, otherwise known as the World's Fair, in St. Louis? It's a fine opportunity, if I say so myself."

Jack looked over at Frances, then at Alexander, but it was hard to read their expressions.

Finally Alexander answered. "Er . . . could you give us a moment to discuss among ourselves?"

"Certainly," replied Zogby. Then he took the medallion back from Frances and tucked it back in his jacket. "I'll be over here." He opened his door, stepped down from the car, and walked off a few yards to wait.

Alexander lowered his voice to a whisper. "What do you think of this fellow's idea?" he asked everyone.

"It's some kind of a scheme," Frances said. "It sounds awfully fishy. *All we have to do* is go to the *World's Fair*? I don't believe it. I think we should just hit the road."

Alexander seemed to agree. "It sounds too good to be true. There's got to be a catch. If carrying some geegaw to St. Louis is such a swell opportunity, why would he give it to a bunch of runaway kids? Why *us*?"

Jack looked out to the road, where dust still hung in the air from the motorcar. Zogby had crossed to the other side of the road to give Jack and the others more privacy, and now he waited patiently.

"Maybe Zogby was once like us," Jack said,

crouching down farther in the car seat so as not to be overheard. "Maybe he made some money for himself and just wants other folks to be able to enjoy the finer things in life." Daniel had been like that—he'd always point out the fanciest buggies and motorcars on Broadway, promising that he'd buy one for the family someday. Jack was sure he would have, too, if he'd lived.

Alexander shrugged. "Eli, what do you think?"

"I don't like that gold thing," Eli said. "I'm not going to carry something with a message on it in some crazy secret language that nobody but the devil can read."

"What, you think it's a curse?" Jack asked.

"Don't know! And not knowing's good enough reason for me not to trust it," Eli replied. "But . . ." He looked thoughtful. "If someone else here wants to carry that thing, I'll gladly go to the Fair."

"Me, too!" Harold put in. "It sounds like the greatest place."

"We're already heading someplace great," Alexander said. "California!"

"But how are we supposed to get there with no money?" Jack argued. "Look, if Mr. Zogby is telling the truth about the reward for the medallion, then we'll continue on to California with some coins in our pockets."

"And if Zogby is lying about the reward?" Frances whispered.

"It'll be the same thing," Jack whispered back. "Except we'll just sell the medallion. It sure looks like it's worth something, doesn't it?"

"It does," Frances admitted, though she was still frowning.

"Maybe we can get some odd jobs at the Fair, too," Eli pointed out. "In fact, I heard some of my mama's cousins were looking to get work there."

"Come on," Jack said to Alexander and Frances. "Doesn't the St. Louis World's Fair sound a whole lot better than just walking down that road?"

Alexander sighed. "Yeah, I guess." But he looked at Frances, as if he were waiting for her to decide.

"Say yes, Frannie?" Harold pleaded.

"*Fine,*" Frances said. "We'll go with Zogby." She opened the door of the motorcar and climbed back in.

Jack couldn't stop the grin from spreading across his face. He stood up in the back seat. "Hey, Mr. Zogby!" he called, waving.

Just for a moment, as Zogby turned to face them,

Jack almost thought it was his brother turning. He had nearly the same kind of dark, slicked-back hair, and he'd pushed his cap back the same way Daniel had done. If Jack needed a sign that this was the right decision—and maybe he did—this was it.

"We'll do it," Jack said. "We'll go to the Fair!"

5
A TICKET TO ST. LOUIS

And just like that, they were back on the road in the motorcar. The noise and jostle of the engine seemed to match Frances's anxious, pounding heartbeat. *What are we doing?* she thought. *And why did Alexander leave it up to* me?

"Excellent!" Zogby had exclaimed when Jack had told him that they'd travel to the Fair in his place. Then he'd reached into his jacket and pulled out a wad of bills. The sight of all that money had made Frances catch her breath. For a moment, all five of them had been too stunned to move as Zogby held out the cash. Finally Alexander had reached out and taken it.

"This is for your fare to St. Louis," Zogby had explained. Then he'd counted out several half-dollar coins. "And these," he had said, dropping the coins into Alexander's hand, "are to get into the Fair. I believe admission is fifty cents a person."

"Thank you, sir," Alexander had managed to say.

At that, Zogby had cranked the engine again for the drive to Hannibal. It was just a couple of miles away, and from there the five of them would journey on to St. Louis.

Now the car was slowing down; they'd passed a sign that said HANNIBAL TOWN LIMITS.

Zogby pulled over and stopped the car on a quiet street at what appeared to be the edge of town. He pointed to an old clapboard hotel on the corner. "Take a right at the Sawyer Inn and then head down the hill until the street ends. You'll see the ticket office right there."

This is all happening so fast, Frances thought as she and her friends climbed out of the car. "Wait, Mr. Zogby," she said, trying to keep her voice from sounding too anxious. "Aren't we supposed to meet someone at the Fair? To give them that gold medal for you?" She pulled out her *Third Eclectic Reader* from her jacket pocket and fished her pencil out of her stocking. "Can you write down their name in here?" she asked, handing him her book.

Zogby nodded and took the pencil. It took a moment for him to find a blank spot—Frances used all the empty spots inside her old schoolbook to make notes of anything she wanted to remember—but then he scrawled something in the corner of the back flyleaf. He gave the book and pencil back to Frances. She was just about to look inside when he snapped his fingers.

"Why, I almost forgot the most important thing!" he said. "Of course I must give you *this*!"

Zogby drew the medallion from his pocket and unwrapped it. He rubbed the edge with his thumb and gathered up the chain. Just before he handed it over, he hesitated briefly; in those few moments Frances thought he looked a little sad, or even sorry about something. But then he wrapped the handkerchief around the medallion and pressed it into Jack's hand.

"Be careful with it," he said.

Jack nodded and tucked the medallion into his hip pocket. Eli, standing right next to him, looked a little relieved when the medallion was put away.

Zogby checked his watch and looked around. "I should really be going. They won't begin boarding for St. Louis for another hour, so you needn't hurry."

But hurrying seemed to be exactly what Zogby himself was doing. He rushed around the side of the motorcar to work the engine crank. "You kids be careful, too," he called.

What does that *mean?* Frances thought. By then the car's motor had started up and Zogby was climbing back into the car.

Frances suddenly remembered the book in her hand. She opened it to see what Zogby had written. There it was, in the corner—a name: *Mr. C. McGee.*

"Wait!" Frances called, but she had to raise her voice over the noise of the engine. "WAIT!"

"WHAT?" Zogby called back.

"WHERE CAN WE FIND MR. McGEE AT THE FAIR?"

Zogby shook his head. "IT'S *MOSES* McGEE," he shouted. Or at least that's what it sounded like to Frances. "MOSES McGEE AT THE TEMPLE OF PROMISES!"

"The Temple of . . . THE TEMPLE OF PROMISES?" *What kind of place is that?*

The young man nodded. "YEP!"

Frances had no idea what *that* meant either. "Moses McGee at the Temple of Promises." It sounded odd, but it was easy enough to remember.

Zogby put the motorcar in gear. "SO LONG," he called. "THANK YOU AND GOOD LUCK!" A cloud of fine dust rose as the young man steered the car into a quick half circle and then drove off in the same direction he'd come in. He turned a corner and was gone.

Jack turned to Frances. "I could've sworn he said the fellow's name was *Mice* McGee," he said. "Not Moses."

Eli shrugged. "Nah, it sounded like 'Moses' to me," he said. "Just like my pop's name."

Frances hadn't been certain about the name either, but Eli sounded sure enough. Yet something still didn't seem right about all this. "What about the 'Temple of Promises'?" she asked. "If you ask me, that sounded even weirder."

Alexander spoke up. "But didn't you hear him talking about all the bizarre things at the Fair? Ostrich farms, golden chariots . . ."

"I suppose you're right," Frances said. Nonetheless, she couldn't stop thinking that *everything* was bizarre right now, not just the Fair. After all, one moment they'd been walking alongside some railroad tracks, and now here they were on their way to St. Louis with at least twenty dollars in their pockets.

Jack and Eli and Alexander started to head down the street Zogby had pointed out, but it wasn't until Harold tugged on her sleeve that Frances realized she hadn't moved.

"Aren't you coming, Frances?" he asked.

"Yes, but . . ." She started walking. "Doesn't anyone else think that everything that just happened was . . . was really *strange*?"

Jack looked at her. "What do you mean?"

"I mean this fellow was simply sitting there in his fancy motorcar in the middle of nowhere! Not even on the road! What was he doing, anyway? And what was he planning on doing before we showed up?"

"Are you saying you think he was up to no good or something?" Eli asked.

"I don't know!" Frances sighed. "It seems a little fishy, that's all. And we're expected to take him at his word and get on a train to—"

"A train!" Harold interrupted, his face crumpling up with worry. "I thought we weren't going to get on another train, Frannie!"

Frances turned to Jack and Eli. "Well, we *weren't*, until we met this Zogby character and all agreed to this half-baked plan. And Harold's right. When we left the Careys' we decided it was too risky to take a train. Who knows—Miss DeHaven might have folks on all the trains looking for us by now."

She got a sick feeling whenever she thought about the cruel woman from the Society for Children's Aid and Relief. Miss Lillian DeHaven had been the chaperone on the orphan train she and Harold and Jack had taken. But she was also the sister of Mrs. Pratcherd, and she'd seen to it that the orphan train children were sent to the Pratcherd Ranch to work long days in the fields.

"Isn't that Miss DeHaven the one who came out to Reverend Carey's farm to check on you?" Eli asked.

"That was her, all right," Jack said. "She *said* she was making sure we were all right. But she had other plans for us. . . ."

"We'd caught her talking about them," Frances continued. She remembered the sound of Miss DeHaven's beautiful but cold voice that day in the Kansas City depot. Frances herself had overheard her talking to the station matron. "She said she was going to send us to a man named Edwin Adolphius, who runs an industrial school. But . . . it didn't sound like a school at all. It sounded like a factory."

"Edwin Adolphius," Eli repeated the name slowly.

"He sounds important. But sometimes, important folks are the worst kind of folks."

"That's for sure," Alexander muttered. "Well, we'll just have to stay on the lookout when we're on the train."

"Speaking of the train, do you suppose it runs along the river?" Jack asked, pointing down the street ahead of them.

They were walking the slope of a gentle hill that Frances now realized was the bank of a very big river. It was in fact the biggest river she'd seen since the Hudson River in New York. It was a great swath of bright silver that glinted under the midday sun.

"The Mississippi," she whispered.

They had come to the bottom of the hill now, where they crossed one more street. Frances studied the row of brick buildings lined up along the river-bank. "I don't see the depot, do you?" she asked the others.

"Zogby mentioned something about a ticket office," Jack said.

Sure enough, there was a sign that said TICKETS on a tiny little structure that was set back behind the other buildings, with a wooden sidewalk and a flight of steps leading up to it.

Alexander was the first to reach the top of the stairs, and as he did, Frances heard him say, "*Whoa! Look at this!*" She ran up the last few steps to see for herself.

They were at the very edge of the river now. And there, along the stretch of bank that had been hidden from view by the buildings, was a huge, white boat. It was bigger than the Staten Island Ferry and grander, too, with three upper decks trimmed with lacy woodwork. It looked to Frances like the fancy layer cakes she'd seen in bakery windows. The two tall chimney pipes trailed smoke as the boat drew nearer to the bank. Frances realized it was heading for the dock near them.

"Are we going on a *ship*?" Harold asked.

"It's a steamboat!" Eli said. "A good old Mississippi steamboat!"

Jack let out a low whistle. "Three decks! That's really something!"

Painted along the side of the boat were the words *Addie Dauphin*. Frances supposed it was the name of the steamboat—it sounded like it was named after someone fun and adventurous, and for a moment she wished she knew this girl, whoever she was. As

Frances stared out across the glittering water at the boat, she felt a thrill unlike any she had felt in days. She was finally glad again to be on the road. *Well, not exactly the road,* she thought. *This time it's the river.*

"Guess what, Harold?" she told her little brother. "Looks like we won't be going on a train after all."

6
THE RIVER RATS

As soon as the *Addie Dauphin* came in, the dock seemed to spring to life. Crews of men strode single file down the gangplanks, carrying crates and bales of straw and cotton. Another team rolled big wooden casks up a ramp to the boat's deck; still more men used ropes and pulleys to haul a load of trunks on board. Jack had been thinking back to New York a lot over the past day, and the dock made him think of the crowded sidewalks of that city—so much hustle back and forth. There was even a group of older boys who loitered by one of the gangplanks, shoving one another jovially the way some of the street-gang kids did back on the Lower East Side.

Jack watched everything, mesmerized, until he felt someone nudge his shoulder.

"Come on, Jack. We've got to get our tickets." Alexander pointed toward the ticket window, where a line had begun to form.

The boys by the gangplank paused their shoving to stare at Jack and the others as they passed. Jack just nodded, the way Daniel had taught him. As he could see that the boys—there were four of them— were only a year or two older than he was. One of them, who seemed to be about Alexander's age, had an unlit cigar stub clamped between his teeth. His eyes had narrowed suddenly, and Jack realized the boy was squinting at Eli.

Some people aren't going to look too kindly on a black boy traveling with you, Eli had said when Jack had invited him to leave the Careys' farm with them. Now Jack understood what Eli meant by "some people"—he could see by the look on this strange boy's face that he was one of those.

Jack met the boy's look with a cold and defiant glare, one that he hoped said, *We don't care what you think.*

Harold, though, was friendlier. "Ahoy!" he called happily to the boys.

The tallest boy in the group grinned. "Whatever you say, kid."

The line at the ticket window had gotten longer. Alexander lined up first since he was holding the money for their fare. Frances and Harold stood behind him, followed by Eli and Jack.

They had been waiting only a few minutes when the man at the ticket window caught sight of them. He scowled, then stood up from his seat and leaned out his window.

"Blasted kids!" he barked at them. "What are you doing?"

Jack froze. He glanced over at the others. They hadn't been doing anything—just standing in line.

"This line is for *first-class* transport!" the man shouted. "Not the likes of you urchins."

The grown-ups ahead of them in line had turned to glare at them. Jack could see that they were certainly dressed first-class—the men in suits and straw boaters, the women in fresh white dresses. Jack looked down at his grubby shirt and dirty fingernails. He and his friends all wore the same things they'd worn for the orphan-train journey, along with a few secondhand items from the Careys, and everything had become dull with dust.

A burly man from the steamboat crew came up

next to them. "You heard him," he said, nodding toward the ticket window. "These folks in line are the *paying* passengers."

Alexander was indignant. "Is that so?" he snapped. He began to reach for his pocket. "Well it just so happens that *we've* got mo—"

Frances grabbed Alexander's hand, stopping him mid-sentence. Jack realized she was trying to keep him from pulling out the money Zogby had given them. She shot Alexander an insistent look that to anyone else might have seemed flirtatious, but, Jack knew, really meant *be quiet.*

"Uh . . ." Alexander said, turning red as Frances kept his hand clasped with hers.

"It just so happens that we've got *no idea* where to board!" Jack said to the burly man. "Is there another line?"

The man pointed toward the end of the dock. "You'll board there, with the rest of the river rats."

He was pointing toward the gangplank where the four older boys waited. Jack realized just then that the rough boys' clothes were at least as worn and dirty as his own—if not more so. To the man, Jack and his friends probably looked just like those boys.

"'River rats'?" Alexander repeated.

"That's what we call you charity cases," the man replied.

Jack's mind raced. *Charity cases*—that must mean those boys were riding for no charge.

"Thank you, sir," Jack told the man. He stepped out of the line and motioned for the others to follow him as he walked down the dock.

"What's going on?" Eli whispered.

"He thinks we're with those other boys and says we should get on the boat with them."

"But Zogby gave us money for first-class tickets," Alexander said.

"Which we can *keep* now!" Frances pointed out. "Who knows when we'll need it?"

"Exactly," Alexander said, even though Jack was pretty sure it was Frances's idea to hold on to the money in the first place.

"Right," Frances muttered, letting go of Alexander's hand. *"Exactly."*

"Can we use the money to buy ice cream at the Fair?" Harold asked.

"Shh!" Frances scolded. "We have to stop talking about the money!"

They were close to the gangplank now, where the four rough boys stood and watched them warily.

One of the boys smirked. "Glad you 'cided to join us," he drawled. He had an accent a little like Eli's, only with more twang in the way he said his *a*'s. Next to him was the tallest boy, who grinned, showing two missing teeth in front. The second tallest boy shrugged and spat, and the fourth one—the boy with the unlit cigar—wouldn't even look at Jack, choosing to stare off into the distance.

Whatever the boy was looking at must have gotten his attention because suddenly his eyes widened. He spat out his cigar and tucked it in his pocket. The other three boys began to appear anxious as well, shuffling their feet and fidgeting. It seemed to Jack that there was someone nearby who was making them uncomfortable.

He turned and saw a man strolling along the dock. A wealthy man, Jack guessed, from the way his suit looked as freshly pressed and crisp as a new handkerchief. His black hair was parted so precisely down the center of his head it was almost painted on, and he had a trim black and silver beard that tapered to a point below his chin. He walked much more slowly than anyone else on the dock, but all the deckhands and crew made a point to stay out of his way.

He smiled at the boys by the gangplank as he passed. A satisfied smile, it seemed to Jack—the kind of smile that he'd seen on folks like the Pratcherds whenever a kid got in trouble at the ranch in Kansas.

"Who's that fellow?" Alexander whispered.

"I don't know," Jack replied. "But I don't like the looks of him."

"Neither do I," said Frances, as she pulled Harold closer to her.

The five of them stood and watched the bearded man walk all the way to the ticket office. Then a long, low whistle sounded, and Jack turned back to see the older boys making their way across the gangplank ramp to board the boat.

"We'd better go," Frances said. She took Harold's hand and led him onto the ramp. Eli followed, and Alexander stepped onto the gangplank after him. Jack meant to as well, but he found himself hesitating, one foot still on the dock.

He looked up at Alexander. "It's funny—it was my idea that we should all go to St. Louis, but now that we're getting on a boat it seems . . . so . . ."

"So final?" Alexander finished.

"Like we're leaving everything else behind. And everyone. All our friends." He thought about the kids who had stayed with the Careys and thought even harder about the ones who they couldn't rescue from the Pratcherds back in Kansas. "It's like we're leaving them behind once and for all."

Alexander tugged Jack's sleeve. "Come on. I don't want to forget our friends either, but you have to start focusing on what's ahead. We haven't left everyone behind—haven't we got Eli with us now?"

Jack nodded. He checked his pocket to make sure the medallion Zogby had given them was still there. Then he started to follow Alexander across the gangplank, which felt unsteady and strange under his feet. The only thing he could do now was keep going.

"And one of these days," Alexander added, "we'll get someplace where we can build Wanderville again."

A bell began to clang, followed by another low whistle, and the boys hurried the rest of the way onto the boat.

Jack took his first step onto the steamboat. He wished the deck felt more like solid ground so that he could feel sure of something. But he didn't feel sure at all.

7
THE LOWER DECK

"Where do we go now, Frannie?" Harold asked once they were aboard the *Addie Dauphin*.

Frances had no idea. She had thought they could follow the older boys, but by the time she'd reached the deck she'd lost track of them.

She and Eli and Harold were on the lowest deck of the steamboat, next to a flight of stairs. Looking up the stairs, Frances could see fancy woodwork in the ceiling, as well as glimpses of the finely dressed passengers gathering up there.

"I reckon they wouldn't let me go up to the higher decks," Eli said warily.

Frances knew that there were places where Eli wasn't allowed just because of his skin color, but this was the first time they'd come across one. "Then we'll just stay down here," she declared. She wasn't going to go anyplace he couldn't.

A few moments later Jack and Alexander had come on board and joined them. Frances turned to grab Harold's hand so that they could all find a place to sit, but he had wandered over to a row of cotton bales in one of the cargo holds.

"These look like big pillows!" he said, scrambling to the top of one of the bales. He flopped over to lie down. "Ow!"

"Get down from there, Harold!" Frances sighed. Alexander reached over and grabbed the boy's belt to help him climb down.

"This one isn't soft at all," Harold complained. "I flopped down on it and it's hard underneath! Like a big box under there!"

Just then Frances felt a big hand on her shoulder. She whirled around and found herself looking up into the face of the burly man they'd seen on the dock.

"This is no playground," he hissed. "Keep that kid away from this cotton. And stay over there by the luggage hold!" He pointed to an area of the lower deck where dozens of trunks were strewn and stacked. "There's benches over there."

Frances stammered a quick thank-you, and she led her four friends to the luggage hold.

It was dim among all the trunks, so it took a moment to make out the four other figures who sat slumped on the rough wooden benches. But Frances knew they had to be the boys they'd seen on the dock.

The tallest boy spoke up. "Well, if it ain't Queenie and her royal court."

Frances just rolled her eyes. "My name's Frances."

"Whatever you say, Your Majesty," the second-tallest boy replied.

Frances knew better than to respond to that. She and Harold sat down in the corner farthest from the older boys, and she set her face in the *I don't care* look that she used to wear whenever she rode the Avenue B Line. Jack and Alexander and Eli pulled up another bench facing Frances and Harold.

"Are they bothering you?" Alexander whispered.

"No," Frances whispered back, and it was the truth. "It's fine."

But that didn't seem to settle Alexander. "Well . . . I'll—I mean, *we'll*—make sure they leave you alone if they bother you."

Frances wondered why Alexander was acting like

some kind of noble prince all of a sudden. "Just ignore them, all right? I'm pretty sure they're ignoring us."

She could see over Alexander's shoulders that the older boys had turned their backs. Two of them seemed to be brothers—the tallest boy and a boy who looked like him except his blond hair was darker. The boy who'd had the cigar in his mouth wore a cap with the brim pushed way back. And the second-tallest boy was barefoot, and the legs of his trousers didn't match because they'd been made from two different worn-out pairs. At first Frances had thought that these boys were hoboes, but there was something about the way they slouched in the dim cargo hold that made her think otherwise. She knew hoboes chose to live the way they did—but with these boys, she wasn't so sure they'd had a choice.

Frances could hear more bells now, ringing from the upper deck, and as the whistle sounded an extralong call, the great steamboat began to move. It chugged slower than a locomotive, and even slower still than Mr. Zogby's automobile. After all that had happened that day, Frances was finally beginning to relax. Harold leaned against her with a soft sigh, too. Everyone seemed to be calmed by the gentle huffing of the great boat's engine.

Everyone, it seemed, except for Eli. He rose from the bench and pulled aside one of the luggage trunks so that he could stand by the deck rail and look out across the water.

Eli didn't say anything at first when Jack came over to stand by him. Together they watched the riverbank go by and the town of Hannibal slip farther away. Jack noticed Eli was holding his mouth tight and biting his lip. Like he was thinking hard about something.

"Eli?" he asked.

But his friend didn't answer.

Jack tried again. "What's wrong?"

"Nothing," Eli muttered, but Jack could tell it was *something*. Frances and the others must have, too, because she and Harold got up from their bench and came over, followed by Alexander. Eli nodded at them in greeting. "Just not sure if I should've left home."

"You mean because of your pa?" Jack asked. He knew that even after everything Eli had been through with his father, it was still hard to say goodbye when they'd left the Careys' farm.

Eli took a deep breath. "My ma would have

wanted me to stay with him. I was all he had after she died."

Jack nodded. Hearing Eli talk about these things always reminded him of his own family. Jack had been sent west to avoid a fate like his brother's, but maybe it would have been better if he'd stayed for his mother's sake. Even if it meant putting up with his own father, who was a lot like Eli's.

He put his hand on Eli's shoulder, and Frances did, too.

After a long silence, it was Harold who finally spoke in a small, soft voice.

"I was sad too when we were at the orphan home," he said. "Because it meant me and Frances didn't have anyone else, or a home, or anything. But now we have Wanderville sometimes." His voice began to get louder and stronger. "Maybe we can have Wanderville right here, so Eli can feel better!"

"Here?" Frances sounded wary. "Here on the *boat*?"

"We're not going to be on the boat very long," Jack said, even though he could see that the idea of rebuilding Wanderville was making Eli smile. *But still* . . . "I doubt we'd have time to build—"

"Why not?" Alexander replied. "Wanderville can be anywhere we want it to be, right? Even on a steamboat."

Harold marched over behind one of the benches and found a spot between two big trunks. "This is the hotel where we can stay. It doesn't even cost anything."

Eli grinned and went to lie down on one of the benches. "Everyone gets their own big bed . . ."

". . . with three pillows," Alexander finished.

Jack started laughing. "What do we do with *three* pillows?"

"One's for sleeping. Two are for throwing!" Frances laughed.

"No, the other two are for your feet," Eli put in. "Haven't you ever had your foot fall asleep?"

By now Harold was standing on one of the benches. "Wanderville has the best bakery!" he called. "Hot buttered rolls, three for a penny!"

"That sounds delicious," Frances said. "What about pie?"

"*Strawberry* pie," Jack added. They'd had some at the Careys' once and it was one of the best things he'd ever tasted. "Only a penny for the whole thing.

And nobody ever kicks you out of the shop for looking in the cases."

"Here we come!" Harold yelled, hopping over to another bench with Eli close behind.

But just then the four older boys stood up and glared from their corner. They pulled three of the benches closer to them so Harold and Eli couldn't use them.

"Aw!" Harold complained. "You're messing everything up!"

"Is that right?" the boy with the patchwork trousers replied. "Just what do you think you're doing in our place?"

"This isn't just *your* place," Alexander muttered.

Jack and Eli stood behind him, keeping an eye on the older boys, who had started to step forward.

The roughest-looking one, who Jack thought of as Cigar Kid, seemed to be sizing up Jack and Eli and Alexander. "Well, we're here, and we're not going anywhere," he said.

"And we want to know what this crazy kid is talking about," the tallest boy replied, pointing to Harold.

"That's my little brother!" Frances shot back.

The tall kid's brother grinned. "And who are *you*, Queenie?"

Frances smirked and crossed her arms defiantly. "I think you answered that question yourself."

Alexander was defiant, too, Jack noticed, but in a way that seemed much more dangerous. His mouth was tight as he stared down all four of the boys.

"Why don't you go jump in the river?" he growled.

Cigar Kid stepped closer. "How about we PUSH you in?" He shoved Alexander. Hard.

Alexander stumbled back a few steps, then squared his shoulders and slammed the boy back.

"*Fight!*" one of the other boys jeered. "Get 'im, Dutch!"

Cigar Kid swung at Alexander, hitting him in the side, but Alexander jabbed an elbow back. Then the barefoot boy stepped up and grabbed Alexander's shirt, pulling him off balance, and Alexander swung at him, and the tall boy, too.

"Hey," Frances said, her voice warning.

"Alex—" Jack called. Alexander was tall and wiry, but he was nuts to try to fight all these boys. Jack felt his hands clench into fists, but he didn't even know where to begin swinging.

Suddenly the tall boy swept his foot out and tripped Alexander, who fell back with a thud.

"*Fight!*" the boys shrieked again.

"Hey!" Frances said. "That's enough."

The boy who was called Dutch tossed his cigar aside, then leapt down and planted his knee right on Alexander's chest. His fists were raised and pulled back. Alexander coughed and sputtered, but his fists were aimed, too.

Oh no, thought Jack. *It's about to get really bad.*

"HEY!" Frances shouted. "I said that's enough!" She barreled forward and shoved Dutch over, then she smacked Alexander's arm. "*Quit it!*" she screamed. "Quit it already! Both of you! *All* of you! DO YOU WANT TO GET THROWN OFF THE BOAT?!"

8
FINN, CHICKS, OWNEY, AND DUTCH

"**I** *said* quit it!" Frances repeated, though by now everyone had fallen silent. They were all staring at her. *It's just like boys*, she thought, *to act like* I'm *the one who's being crazy*. "I swear we'll get kicked off this boat if you fools keep fighting and scrapping around like a pack of stray dogs!"

She crossed her arms and glared at Alexander, then at Dutch and his three friends. She even shot a cold look her little brother's way, just in case he ever decided getting into fisticuffs was a good idea.

"They started it," Harold mumbled, pointing to the older boys.

The tallest boy protested. "We wasn't trying to start anything! We was just wondering what you all was doing!"

"Yeah!" his shorter brother put in. "What were you all talking about? What's with this *Wandervale* place?"

Frances didn't know what to say. But Alexander, who was still lying back on the deck where he'd fallen, suddenly sat up straight, and his face brightened.

"You mean . . . Wanderville?" he asked.

The four older boys all nodded, and they leaned in expectantly.

This time it was Harold who spoke up. "Wanderville is a town and we live there sometimes. That's where we were going!"

"It sounds real nice," the barefoot boy said. He exchanged a look with his other three friends, as if they were all deciding something. "Are you . . . er, *still* going there?"

"Of course!" Alexander replied. "And Wanderville is open to any kid who needs a place to go. Or any kid in need of freedom."

They were all quiet for a moment. When she and Harold and the others had been "building" Wanderville a few minutes ago, Frances had noticed the older boys observing them. They'd feigned bored expressions, but they'd watched so intently she knew they were curious. Maybe even jealous.

Finally, the boy named Dutch cleared his throat. "Could, uh . . . could we go to Wanderville, too?" he asked. He had pulled out another cigar stub from his pocket and was picking at it nervously.

Frances glanced over at Jack and Eli, who both looked surprised, then to Harold, who appeared to be holding his breath, and finally to Alexander, who was nodding his head excitedly.

"Sure!" he said.

Frances could feel herself grinning, too.

The boy reached out his hand and helped Alexander up. "Guess you already heard my name's Dutch," he said. Then he pointed to his friends. "This here's Finn," he said, indicating the tallest boy. "And his brother's Chester, but we call 'im Chicks."

Chicks was the one with darker blond hair, and Frances felt satisfied that she'd guessed he and Finn were siblings.

"And this here is Owney," Dutch said, motioning to the barefoot boy with the trousers that had been sewn together. Though as Frances looked closer at all four of the boys, she could see how threadbare *all* their clothes were. While the things she and her friends wore were a little shabby, the shirts and trousers on these boys had been mended again and again.

Still, when it was her turn to introduce herself, they all tilted their heads politely. They weren't completely wild, Frances realized. All the same, she noticed Alexander and Jack checking their pockets when they thought the other boys weren't looking to make sure the money and the medallion Zogby had given them were safe.

Once all the introductions had been made, Harold added, "My traveling name is 'Tomato Can'!"

Finn smiled at that. "*Travelin' name,* huh?"

"The hoboes gave me that name when we rode the rails," Harold bragged.

"Really?" asked Owney. "You rode the rails with hoboes?"

Chicks turned to Jack. "Are you all runaways or something?"

"In a way," Jack said, and he explained how he, Frances, Harold, and Alexander had come out from New York City on orphan trains, then been forced to work at the Pratcherds' before they'd finally escaped. Once he was done, Eli told his own story about having to work in the fields so much he couldn't go to school.

Dutch had lost his scowl. "I reckoned we all had something in common. Me and my chums here have been working our hides off for the past two years!"

"We was all at a broom factory for a while," said Finn. "Wrapping bundles of straw with wire all day long."

"The straw was worse than the wire," Chicks added. "It was all wet and smelled bad."

Everyone listened as the other two older boys joined in with their stories, too. After the broom factory, Owney told them, they'd been sent to a glasswork, where they'd had to run carrying hot molds of molten glass.

"We worked in the middle of the night," Dutch said. "And we had to run fast. Owney, show 'em your burn."

Owney rolled up his sleeve to show a terrible puckered scar on the inside of his arm.

"I was carrying a mold, and I tripped," he said.

Frances gasped in surprise, and so did Eli. "Why did you have to work in such an awful place?" she asked.

Owney looked down at his bare feet. "My family got debts to pay."

"So does mine," Dutch muttered. "There's a man who loaned my pa money when our crops didn't come in. But my folks don't have a dime to pay him back, so the man made me go to the broom factory and now he takes my wages." He motioned over to Finn and Chicks. "It's the same thing with their mama."

Frances couldn't believe it. These boys had parents—but they were taken away from them to work. "Do you miss home?" she asked.

Finn and Chicks looked at each other. "A little," said Finn. "But even if our ma didn't owe money, there was too many mouths to feed."

"I ain't ever going home again," Dutch said matter-of-factly.

"Me neither," Owney said. "It ain't fair that I have to work off something that wasn't my fault."

"I can't even imagine how rough it's all been," Frances said softly. Jack and Eli nodded in agreement.

Dutch gave a half smile and winked at Frances. "Aw, we're tough."

As Frances smiled back, she thought she could see, from the corner of her eye, Alexander scowling, but when she turned to face him he simply shrugged.

"But speaking of work." Finn looked around nervously. "We're supposed to be working right now." He stepped over to a row of steamer trunks: his brother and their two friends followed.

"Here?" Alexander asked. "On the boat?"

Dutch nodded and picked up one of the trunks.

"Yep, here in the cargo hold. Don't want to be caught loafing." He stacked the trunk he was carrying, and then took another trunk from Chicks and added it to the stack.

"We'll help," Jack said, grabbing a trunk. "What should we do?"

"Stack all the trunks up and tie 'em so they stay in place," Finn said. "That's what we were told to do. The fellow givin' orders said we needed to make more space in the luggage hold by tonight."

"That's odd," Frances said. She remembered a sign on the ticket window in Hannibal that said EXPRESS PASSAGE TO ST. LOUIS. She knew it meant the boat wouldn't be making any more stops. "We're going straight to St. Louis. We'll be there tomorrow. Why would they need room tonight?"

Owney shrugged and tugged at a thread on his trousers. "Beats me."

All nine of them began to work together, stacking trunks and tying them with rope, securing them to iron rings that were fastened to the deck. Some of the trunks weren't very heavy, and the older boys could stack them all the way to the ceiling.

"At least *this* work isn't too hard," Jack remarked

to the boys. "Compared to those other places you've been."

"That's true," Finn said. But even though Frances had noticed Finn was the one who smiled the most, his face was solemn now. "Only thing is . . ." he began, but his voice trailed off.

His brother finished. "Only thing is, we're on our way to another factory. And we heard it's even worse than the ones from before. In fact . . . folks say it's the worst place of all."

What could be worse than a place where you get burned by hot glass? Frances thought.

"It's a cannery," Owney said, bringing his voice down to a near whisper. "For packing things in tin cans. Sardines, tomatoes. My cousin was there. Says everything is scalding hot and it stinks of fish. You cut fish up all day and brine it, and your hands get all cut and sore from the salt." He looked down at his hands, then rolled his sleeve back down over the scar on his arm.

"Adolphius Canning, the place is called," Dutch continued. "And the fellow who owns it is on board! He's the boss of everyone!"

Frances nearly stopped breathing. She looked

over at Jack. He had been standing on one of the benches tying down one of the taller stacks. But he had frozen the sound of the name.

It was Alexander who finally spoke. *"Edwin Adolphius?"*

Eli's eyes had gone wide with recognition. "Isn't that the man you were talking about, Frances? The one Miss DeHaven was going to send you to?"

"Yes," she whispered.

Jack still hadn't moved. "He's *here*, on this boat?"

"You didn't know?" Chicks asked. "But you saw him on the docks, same as we did. He walked right by us."

It was the man with the black and silver beard, Frances realized. The one with the fine suit and the smug smile who'd strolled past just before they'd boarded. "But I don't understand," she said. "What's he doing here?"

"That's the worst part," Finn said. "This whole place belongs to Edwin Adolphius! This is *his* steamboat."

One of the trunks that Jack had been trying to tie down slipped off the stack just then and hit the deck. To Frances it sounded like a clap of thunder—*bam!*— from a storm that was suddenly much too close.

9
A CERTAIN FIRST-CLASS PASSENGER

The steamer trunk lay on its side where it had fallen. The brass lock swung loose and the lid had pulled open.

"If that thing's broken we'll get a thrashing for sure," Dutch said, a nervous edge in his voice.

"It's my fault," Jack said as he stepped down from the bench and set the trunk proper. "So I'm the only one who ought to be thrashed."

Owney had come over to help. "Well, today's your lucky day," he said, nudging the trunk with his bare foot and looking under the lid. "It ain't broken. What's more, it ain't even got nothing in it."

Jack blinked in surprise. "Really?" But sure enough, he peered inside and the trunk was indeed completely empty.

"I thought some of those trunks felt awfully light," Eli said.

Finn nodded and picked up one of the other trunks nearby. "A whole lot of them over here in this corner feel like they're empty, too. Like this one." He slammed it down on the ground and it made a loud but hollow noise.

"Quit throwing those things!" Dutch snapped. "Do you want to get in trouble?"

Suddenly Chicks leapt down from the bench he'd been standing on. "Someone's coming!" he hissed.

Jack heard footsteps along the deck, coming closer. But they weren't the sort of heavy noise made by boots. They were hard little taps instead.

Owney and Frances stood on their toes to peek over one of the stacks of trunks at the person who was approaching.

"Ugh," Owney said, rolling his eyes. "It's her."

"*It's her,*" Frances repeated, stunned. Then she turned and her eyes met Jack's. "Quick, hide!"

Dutch and the other boys looked confused. "Huh?" Dutch muttered.

"*We* have to hide!" she gasped. "Now!" She reached for Harold and grabbed his wrist, and they scurried between two stacks of trunks until they were out of sight. Alexander seemed to understand, too, and he went in after them. Jack wasn't sure *he* understood, but he motioned for Eli to follow him and Alexander.

"What's going on?" Eli whispered as they crawled into the dark space behind the trunks.

Jack couldn't answer. He could only put his finger to his lips to indicate *be quiet.* But it was anything but quiet inside his head. *It can't possibly be her,* he thought. *It can't be!* Yet Jack figured there could be only one reason why Frances would look so scared.

"How can *she* be *here?*" he said under his breath.

"*Who?*" Eli asked.

Just then Jack heard a voice speaking to the older boys. A voice that he knew could be sweet sounding but could also be flat and cruel and cold. . . .

"I suppose you boys are *enjoying* your little journey."

Miss DeHaven.

Jack peeked out to get a better view—it really *was* her! She stood next to the deck railing in the late afternoon sunlight. She was more elegantly dressed than he'd ever seen her—her shoulders were bare, and she was wearing a fancy black gown with beads and scalloped trimmings that reminded Jack of serpents' scales.

She was one of the finely dressed passengers who traveled on the upper decks, Jack realized. *Why did she come down here?*

Frances and Alexander had found places alongside Jack to peek out at the scene just beyond their hiding spot.

Miss DeHaven looked the older boys up and down. "With all this racket," she told them, "it would seem that you're enjoying the trip a little *too* much."

"S-sorry, ma'am," Finn stammered.

Jack couldn't see his face from where he was hiding, but his shoulders were tense and he stood as if frozen in place. All the boys looked on edge.

"*Sorry, ma'am,*" replied Miss DeHaven in a sneering imitation of Finn. "Spoken like a servant boy! Perhaps there's *hope* for you *yet.*"

Finn reminded silent, though he nodded.

"The *rest* of you," Miss DeHaven continued, "appear too lowborn for that sort of work. But *happily,* we have found suitable positions for all of you, you know."

The four older boys were looking down at their

feet now. Jack sensed that they'd had to endure Miss DeHaven before.

"And *this* time it better work out," she said. "No more getting yourself into clumsy little *predicaments* to shirk your duties."

As she spoke, she looked over at Owney, who rubbed his scarred arm self-consciously.

"Yes, ma'am," he mumbled.

A bell clanged from the upper decks, and Miss DeHaven smirked and gathered the skirt of her fine gown. "*So* delightful to have this *visit*," she said, her voice becoming more silvery and musical, as if she was suddenly someone else.

Her shoes tapped along the deck and then up the iron steps to the next deck above them. Jack listened hard until he couldn't hear them any more.

"You can come out now," Owney called.

Alexander was the first one to emerge. "You know Miss DeHaven?" he asked the older boys incredulously.

"She was on our orphan train," Jack added.

"Is that what her name is?" Dutch said. "She started showing up at the glass factory saying she had to 'check on us.' At first we all thought that meant she *cared* or something. . . ."

"But all she would do was go on and on about hard work and how lucky we were to be working," Finn added.

"She's the worst," said Owney. "Even if she is awful pretty."

Harold shook his head. "She's awful *awful.*"

The older boys laughed. "Ha, she sure is!" Chicks said with a snicker.

"What are you laughing at?" Alexander said, his voice suddenly icy. "This isn't a joke. Miss DeHaven is our *enemy.* I can't believe anyone would ever think she's pretty." He was pacing around the deck, his hands clenching. *Keep your head,* Jack wanted to tell him.

"Settle down, buddy," Finn warned.

"Besides," Dutch said, grinning at Frances. "We never said she was prettier than Queenie over here."

Frances choked back a laugh and swatted Dutch's arm. "Quit calling me *Queenie!*" she said, though Jack suspected she didn't much mind at all.

"Yeah, quit calling her that, all of you!" Alexander sputtered at the older boys. "Leave her alone!"

Uh-oh, Jack thought.

"They're not bothering me, *Alexander,*" Frances said pointedly.

"Well, you shouldn't talk to them!" he snapped, his face getting redder. "How do you know they're really on our side and not Miss DeHaven's? That they're not just telling us some story?"

Owney's eyes flashed. "We ain't lying, if that's what you mean!"

"Alexander, you're being *ridiculous!*" Frances fired back. "And don't you *dare* tell me who I should or shouldn't talk to!"

She turned around abruptly, her back to Alexander.

Jack stepped in between them. "Alex," he said, his voice low. "Just calm down."

But Alexander just stomped off in the opposite direction. He turned a corner and disappeared.

Finn nodded. "Looks like someone needs to cool his stew."

Frances glanced at Jack. "Should we go after him?"

Jack shook his head. "We ought to leave him alone for now. Let him think."

But, Jack thought, *he's not the only one with a lot on his mind.*

10
A LITTLE TASTE OF CALIFORNIA

*W*hat *kind of a name is "Chicks"?* Alexander thought to himself. *Or "Owney"?* He paced back and forth on the deck.

He'd come all the way over to the other side of the *Addie Dauphin* to clear his head, but it was no use: His head was still too full of annoying questions, like, *What kind of fool would name a kid "Dutch?"* and, *Is Dutch even Dutch?* Alexander also wondered what country the Dutch came from. He wondered if he was supposed to have learned that in school. He wondered if Frances knew.

He paced back and forth some more, then he stood and watched the great big paddle wheel that churned up water in back of the boat. It went around and around like the thoughts in his head.

The thing he wondered the most was: *What if Frances likes them better than me?* That was the worst question of all. He couldn't believe she didn't mind when those older boys called her "Queenie" and "Your Majesty." Once, back at the Careys' farm, he'd called her "Fancy," just as a joke, and she'd kicked him in the shin. What did those boys have that he didn't have? At least *he* had all his teeth, he thought, unlike that Finn kid. . . .

A steady breeze was blowing across the deck. His face had been too angry-hot to notice it at first, but now it felt cool and gentle. Alexander unclenched his hands and stretched his arms. He was beginning to feel better, in a mood to explore, even, so when he saw a short ladder leading up to another cargo hold, he climbed it and peered in at the rows of barrels and boxes.

He caught glimpses of bright yellow between the slats of some of the crates. No, not yellow—a deeper color. He went to get a closer look. *Could they be?* He could smell them—a perfumey scent that was sweet and sharp. He tugged at the crate slats until he found a loose one and pulled it forward, and then he could see for sure.

Oranges! One of them rolled out and fell right into

his hand. It was fresh and peeled easily. Alexander broke off a section of the delicious fruit and popped it into his mouth.

"It has to be a sign," he said under his breath. A sign, he thought, that they would make it out west. Hadn't he'd been promising oranges in California to the citizens of Wanderville?

He pulled two more oranges free from the crates and stuffed them in the sleeves of his jacket. *Wait till everyone sees these,* he thought. *Especially Frances.* She'd be so happy and remember that he was the one who first built Wanderville. And she'd forget those boys. As Alexander climbed back down the cargo ladder he was in such good spirits he felt like he could just leap off the last step and keep walking on air.

As he started to make his way back to the luggage hold where his friends were, he passed a set of narrow stairs, which gave him another idea: Why not get a peek of the deck above and tell the others about it? The upper decks had to be grander. Maybe there was even some more food up there he could liberate. Oranges weren't enough for a full meal, after all. He crept up the stairs carefully so as not to make noise and tiptoed down a narrow passageway.

The passage ended at a great, long parlor that smelled of both cigar smoke and perfume. The polished woodwork gleamed, and there were ferns in brass vases and a thick Oriental carpet on the floor. Alexander's footsteps were silent as he trod on it, and for a moment it made him feel like he'd become a ghost. But he knew that here, more than ever, he'd have to be careful to escape notice. All the finely dressed passengers were in this section—portly men gathered around card tables, the chairs and divans filled with women who fanned themselves or gazed out the windows. The sky above the riverbank was turning pink—it must have been early evening—and Alexander supposed everyone was dressed for dinner.

He found a tall chair to stand behind. There was no use hiding in this room, but the top of the chair came almost to his shoulders and he could conceal his worn, dusty jacket. The trick to being in places like this, Alexander knew, was to act like he was supposed to be there. He'd done the same thing back at the mercantile in Kansas where he'd taken things that Wanderville needed. *Nothing to it,* he thought.

He glanced around and spotted a platter of jam sandwiches that had been cut into tiny triangles.

He knew he'd be able to slip a few of those into his sleeve, if he could just make his way over. . . .

Just then a voice seemed to rise up over the murmur of the crowd.

"But *of course,* dear *Edwin.* It would be a *lovely* excursion!"

Alexander tried not to shudder. Miss DeHaven was just a few feet away!

She sat at a little table next to the bearded man, the one they'd seen at the dock. The man the older boys said was Edwin Adolphius. Miss DeHaven had just called him *Edwin,* too.

Alexander's mind raced. The chair that he stood behind was made of painted wicker, with a high, latticed back like a screen. He slowly moved the chair so that its back was to Miss DeHaven's table, and then he sat down. The chair was tall enough to completely hide him, but when he turned his head to the side he could peer out through the little openings in the latticework. He could see them both now: Mr. Adolphius was pouring a drink for Miss DeHaven—some kind of amber cordial served in tiny little glasses shaped like tulips—and bragging about his motorcar.

"Let me tell you, it drives so smooth that they say a lady could take the wheel. Why, I'll even let you try!" Mr. Adolphius declared. Alexander could tell he was the kind of man who never noticed that his voice was always just a bit too loud.

"Perhaps I shall," Miss DeHaven replied. "I hope it won't be too *difficult*."

Alexander suspected that Miss DeHaven was more clever than Mr. Adolphius, who tried to act refined but was really sort of coarse, and that she was trying to humor him.

"Won't be hard at all, Miss Lillian!" Mr. Adolphius replied. "After all, you sure know how to handle those charity cases! Those boys are uncorkable, but a year or two of cannery packing will shut them right up."

"I *think* you mean *incorrigible*, Edwin. Not *uncorkable*," said Miss DeHaven. "And don't forget to call it an industrial school instead of a cannery. Because are they not *learning* to be *industrious*, these wretched boys? Educating *themselves* about the rigors of work while they have the *great privilege* of *helping* you?" She picked up her glass and sipped it.

Edwin Adolphius grinned. "I like how you say that!" he boomed. "Industrial school sure sounds better than packing tins with fish guts."

Miss DeHaven made a face. "Indeed it does. And

I am *happy* to help you find *students* and escort them to the factory in St. Louis. And as a matter of *fact . . .*" She let her voice trail off while she slowly traced her finger around the rim of her glass.

"Yes?" Mr. Adolphius murmured. "What is it?"

Alexander could tell the fellow was entranced by Miss DeHaven. He supposed she *was* pretty, like Owney had said. Was Frances prettier? Alexander didn't know. With Frances, it wasn't about "pretty," the way he liked her. He hoped he wouldn't ever make a fool of himself in front of Frances the way Mr. Adolphius was doing right now, gazing at Miss DeHaven like she was made of pure gold.

Miss DeHaven seemed to enjoy the attention. "As a *matter* of fact, Edwin," she said. "I know of some *orphans* who would be *perfect* students. It's been *so* very hard finding an *ideal* placement for them. They have an *unfortunate* tendency to run away."

Alexander froze in his seat. Was she talking about *them*? He wasn't sure. Either way, he knew he had to get out of the room. He stood, but stayed crouched behind the chair.

"Well, I'll make sure they don't run away from the canning factory," Mr. Adolphius remarked.

"Yes, but I'll just have to *find* them first," Miss

DeHaven replied. "They absconded from a farm near Bremerton. . . ." She was no longer trying to speak in a pleasant voice.

And now, Alexander *knew* she was talking about them. *How did she know we left the Careys' farm?* he wondered. He tried to stay hunched down as he moved toward the doorway.

". . . but I have reason to believe they're still in Missouri," she added.

He was close to the doorway now. *Just a few more steps.* He could just make out the outline of Miss DeHaven from the corner of his eye. She'd had her head turned in the opposite direction a few moments before, and if she stayed that way, he'd be safe.

He just needed to make sure . . . he turned to look, just for a second . . . and found that Miss DeHaven was staring right at him.

He darted out the door, his face hot. *She didn't recognize me,* he told himself. *It was just for a moment. Right?*

Alexander could hear Mr. Adolphius, his voice too loud as usual. "We'll find them!"

The words rang in Alexander's ears as he ran down the stairs and all the way back across the lower deck.

11
THE FRUIT OF THEIR LABORS

The mood on the lower deck had changed now that Alexander was elsewhere and there was no more work to be done in the cargo hold. The sun hung lower over the river and they could all hear piano music clinking gently from one of the upper decks. The older boys formed a little square as they sat cross-legged on the deck playing cards, while Frances stood with Harold and Eli at the railing, taking in the view.

"It's nice, isn't it?" Frances murmured. The river was one wide stripe of silvery blue, and then above it the deep green stripe of the riverbank trees, and finally the brighter blue of the sky.

"It's so slow," Harold said listlessly. "Not like the train." He wiped his nose on his sleeve. Frances had seen him do that twice already today, and she was starting to worry that he was getting one of his colds again.

"Sometimes slow is good," Eli said. "Remember Ora, back at the Careys? Well, she used to tell all about a rabbit and a Mississippi mud turtle that ran a race. . . ."

"Yeah?" Harold said, perking up a little as Eli began to tell the story.

Frances had read Harold every poem or tale in the *Third Eclectic Reader* at least four times, so she was grateful that Eli had all these new stories and could tell them so well, even doing different voices for the animal characters. The tale he was telling now was so entertaining that the older boys put down their cards and scooted closer to listen.

Frances looked around for Jack. She found him sitting on the deck against one of the trunks, out of sight of the older boys. As she sat down next to him, she noticed he had taken out the medallion that Zogby had given them and was turning it over in his hands, studying it.

"Can I look at it, too?" she asked. Jack nodded and handed it to her.

She spent a long time peering closely at the little

images carved in gold—the bird on one side and the beast on the other side. Was it a cow? An ox?

"This thing is so weird," she said. "I wonder what it's for."

"Telling fortunes, maybe?" Jack suggested.

"We should rub it and ask it about the future or something," Frances said. She didn't really believe in that sort of thing, but she thought maybe if she just knew the medallion's purpose she wouldn't think it was so creepy. "Should we ask it about California?" She laughed.

But Jack didn't answer or even laugh. And when Frances had said *California* he'd looked away. *What's going on?*

"Okay, Jack," she said finally. "What is it?"

"Maybe . . ." Jack began. "Maybe I won't go to California with the rest of you."

"*What?* Why?"

"I've just been thinking it might be better if I went back to New York," Jack said. "It seems like the more I try to save other kids, the worse things get, and I don't want them to get bad for you too." He was talking faster now, the words tumbling out. "I could look for my family. Maybe my father would want me again."

Frances looked him in the eyes. "*Jack*. Stop thinking this way. Are you sure you want to leave? Or that your folks would want you back?"

"No," Jack said. "I'm not sure at all. But the only way I can be sure is if I go."

Frances shook her head. She knew what it was like to be all on your own in New York. And there was a good chance that this could be Jack's fate as well.

"It won't be the same there, Jack," she said.

"I suppose," Jack replied. "But maybe after the Fair I could find a train back to New York and—"

Another voice spoke up. "And you'll *what*?"

Frances turned to see Eli standing there. He must have been walking over to see them and had overheard the conversation.

"It's nothing," Jack started to say. "I was just thinking . . ."

Eli cut in. "Yeah, well, *I* was thinking, too. Thinking about whether I ought to look for my mama's cousins in St. Louis. 'Cause even though I don't know them so well they're part of the family I was born to. But the thing is," he said, looking straight at Jack, "I thought Wanderville was going to be my family now. Everyone in it, I mean. Is that still true?"

"Of course it's true," Frances said. "Isn't that right, Jack?"

Jack didn't say anything for a moment. Then he took a deep breath and nodded. "Right," he said. "We've got Wanderville, no matter what."

That seemed to satisfy Eli. But Frances suspected Jack wanted to say more: *We've got Wanderville, but . . .*

Instead, though, Jack changed the subject. "And we've got *this,* too!" he exclaimed, grabbing the medallion back from Frances and grinning big. "Our ticket to the World's Fair. It's really something, isn't it?"

Frances tried to smile back. "It sure is," she said.

Only now she wished for real that the medallion could tell them the future. That way she'd know what Jack was going to do.

Jack still didn't quite trust the older boys, but at least they had gotten friendlier as they all whiled away the afternoon in the luggage hold. The boys had liked Eli's stories, and then Owney volunteered to tell one, too—a cowboy story from a dime novel he'd heard read aloud at the broom factory. It was a pretty exciting tale about bank robbers making a daring escape.

"The robbers ordered everyone out of the stage-coach," Owney told them. "Then they took their trunks and emptied them out right there on the road!"

"Why'd they do that?" Harold wondered. "That's mean!"

"So they could have a place to hide the gold they stole from the bank," Owney explained as he tugged at a loose thread on his patchwork trousers. "And then the robbers could disguise themselves as regular old stagecoach drivers."

"Oh," Harold said, wiping his nose on his sleeve again. He seemed to be thinking. "Do you think anyone is hiding gold in *those*?" he asked, pointing over to the trunks they'd just stacked.

Chicks laughed. "Naw, probably not. But someone sure could hide something in those if they really wanted to."

Jack couldn't help thinking there was something very strange about those empty trunks. But he didn't know what, exactly. He was about to say something when suddenly Frances stood up in surprise.

"Hey! You're back!" she said.

Jack turned to look behind him. There was Alexander, nodding slowly. He was slightly out of breath, and he looked a little sick, too. Not green in the face, exactly, but ashen. Like he'd seen a ghost.

"Are you okay?" Jack asked him. Alexander never looked that grim unless it was about something big.

Alexander shook his head.

Frances stepped closer. "Alex, what's wrong?"

"I just saw . . ." Alexander began. But then he shook his head again. He took a deep breath. "Nothing's wrong!" he said, his voice suddenly brighter. "Look!" He reached up his sleeve and pulled out an orange. "See what I found!"

Finn's eyes got wide. "*Oranges?* Where'd you get those?"

"Never had a whole orange before," said Owney.

"Well, here you go," Alexander said, tossing the fruit to Owney. Then he pulled out two more oranges, giving one to Harold and handing the other, with an elegant bow, to Frances.

Dutch had his unlit cigar clenched in his teeth again, and he pushed it to the other side of his mouth so that he could sneer. "I suppose you went a-begging on the upper decks?" he asked Alexander. "Sang a little song, did you?"

Alexander seemed to tense up. "Not at all," he

replied. He turned to take a quick look behind him, then he lowered his voice. "Look, there's plenty more oranges where those came from. I'll . . . I'll show you."

"What if we get caught?" Chicks asked, glancing at his brother.

"We won't," Alexander shot back. "There's nobody around there. Come on!" He was talking fast now, his voice insistent. Jack hoped Alexander knew what he was talking about.

They all followed Alexander over to the other side of the lower deck, and he showed them where a short ladder led into a little room filled with crates. He walked up to one and pulled a slat aside, and three oranges rolled right out onto the floor.

"Wow!" Dutch said under his breath. He and Finn snatched them up while Chicks reached into the crate to grab more. Meanwhile Alexander opened up another crate for Eli and Owney. Jack slipped an orange into his pocket, then another. It still felt strange to Jack to "liberate" things, but it was hard to say no to a good orange, which you could keep for days and which could be eaten when you were both hungry and thirsty.

"Try 'em," Eli urged. He'd peeled one open and was popping the juicy sections into his mouth. "They're good!"

Harold was sitting on the deck with a pile of orange peels in his lap, his face sticky and flushed and happy.

Frances beamed at him and turned to Jack and Alexander. "He ate the whole thing. And look at him—he looks better than he has in days. Oranges are just what he needs right now."

"Frannie, can I have another?" Harold called.

"Of course!" Frances said. She retrieved one from the crate and handed it to her brother. Then she bounded over to Alexander and hugged him. "Thank you so much!" she told him.

Jack could see Alexander grinning over Frances's shoulder. *He sure looks proud of himself.*

They all soon realized they could fit only a few oranges each in their pockets, so they decided to eat as many as they could there in the cargo hold.

"We need a place to hide the peelings, though," Eli noted.

"We can use that trunk in the corner," Chicks said, pointing to one that stood open and empty behind some of the crates.

Jack went over to the trunk to toss out his peels and noticed that there were marks carved in the wood trim. There were little hash lines, crossed off in groups of five, as if someone had marked days or hours; a word all in caps—*PAZ*; and then some other marks that weren't letters or numbers.

They looked, in fact, like the markings on the medallion Zogby had given them! One he knew for sure—a little circle with two points on top. It resembled a loop of string with two loose ends. There was also one that looked like a letter *M* with a downward-pointing arrow.

He wanted to show Alexander and Frances. But Alexander was busy playing catch with Owney, tossing one of the oranges back and forth. "Hey," Jack said, trying to wave Alexander over between tosses.

"What?" Alexander said. At that very same moment, Owney threw the orange back. It sailed past Alexander before he had a chance to catch it. It bounced once at the door to the cargo hold, then dropped down over the short ladder to the deck.

"Get it quick!" Dutch said. "Nobody should know we're in here!"

Jack leapt down the ladder with the others close behind. He spotted the orange rolling along the deck and scrambled to retrieve it. By the time he reached it, though, something had stopped its rolling. Or rather, *someone*. Someone with fine black shoes—gentleman's shoes—that were so clean they gleamed.

Jack felt a chill. He had a feeling he knew whose shoes these were. He looked up and saw that he'd guessed correctly.

Because he was looking right into the furious face of Mr. Edwin Adolphius.

12
BOUND FOR THE FACTORY!

"Are we in jail now?" Harold whispered.

"Of course not," Frances whispered back. "There's no jail on a boat. This is just a pen for animals. See all the straw?"

Still, she had to admit that the tiny pen near the back of the steamboat seemed a lot like a jail cell, with iron bars that went all the way to the ceiling. It didn't help that the sun had set for the evening, and the lamp in the corridor threw all kinds of strange shadows.

Owney touched the bars grimly. "Bet they built it this way for the goats. So's they won't chew their way out."

Frances sighed. Not even *goats* wanted to be in this place, which was dark and smelly, with only bales of straw for sitting. She sank down glumly next to Harold on one scratchy bale. The older boys, Eli, and Alexander had found spots on the floor, but Jack stood by the entrance. He glared out at Edwin Adolphius and the three mean-looking deckhands who had shoved them one by one into the pen.

"You have no right to keep us here!" Jack growled.

"I have *every* right!" Mr. Adolphius spat. "You kids are stowaways and thieves. You've trespassed on my property and stolen from me!"

"They're just oranges," Frances muttered.

Mr. Adolphius narrowed his eyes. "*Them* oranges," he said, "are meant to be *canned*. They're headed to my factory. Just like you and your grubby little friends, *girl*."

The words hit Frances like a blow. "*What?*" she whispered. She turned to Alexander and saw his face had gone ashen again, just like it had when he'd come back from his excursion.

"What are you talking about?" Jack asked Mr. Adolphius, his voice becoming frantic.

Edwin Adolphius just smiled and cocked his head. "I think I hear your chaperone coming. I'll let *her* explain."

Even though Frances recognized the hard, small

footsteps that tapped their way along the boards of the deck, she still wasn't quite prepared to see Miss DeHaven's gloating face. Would she ever be?

"My *dear* children," Miss DeHaven said. "I *do* hope your new accommodations are satisfactory."

"What's going on?" Jack demanded.

"Why, you're the luckiest children to ever stow away on a steamboat! Despite all your *criminal* actions, Mr. Adolphius has graciously agreed to admit you to his industrial school, where you'll be joining *these*"—she motioned toward the four older boys—"most *fortunate* lads." Dutch glowered at Miss DeHaven, but she just smirked and continued. "All of you are being given a *wonderful* opportunity! I'm *so* glad."

Frances knew that Miss DeHaven liked to say things that were the opposite of what they really meant. But she had a feeling that for once Miss DeHaven really *was* glad that they were being sent to "industrial school."

"It's not really a *school*, is it?" Frances said bitterly. "It's just an awful canning factory, isn't it?"

Miss DeHaven's face seemed to twitch a little at the question. *Doesn't she ever get tired of lying?* Frances thought.

But then the woman seemed to compose herself. She smiled sweetly and pointed to Alexander. "Of *course* it's a school. Why, your friend here heard me and Mr. Adolphius talking all about it when he stole up to the first-class deck! He heard all about how much I wanted to *find* you poor children again and send you someplace where you could *learn a lesson.* He knows how much I want to *help.*"

Alexander, who had been silent this whole time, suddenly sprang to his feet and leaned against the bars next to Jack. "This isn't 'help,' and *you know it*!" he screamed.

But Miss DeHaven was already walking away down the corridor, followed by Mr. Adolphius and the deckhands.

Frances felt her face get hot. She couldn't believe how Alexander had misled them. "You knew what Miss DeHaven was planning?" she asked him.

"And you *didn't tell us*?" Jack added.

Alexander sighed. "I didn't know how to tell you."

"If we'd known, we would have laid low and stayed hidden all the way to St. Louis, instead of raiding a bunch of silly orange crates," Jack said, pacing back and forth. "It's just like you to decide things for us without giving us any say."

Jack and Alexander fought about this kind of thing all the time, Frances knew. But Jack was right. Alexander had been foolish, and selfish, too.

"I'm sorry," Alexander said weakly. But Jack sat down next to Eli and turned his back. Frances put her arm around Harold and wouldn't look at Alexander.

She heard him sit down next to the older boys. "I suppose you're mad at me, too?" he asked them.

Out of the corner of her eye she could see Dutch shrugging. "Nope."

"Really?"

"Ain't much worse for us than it's always been," Owney said. He'd pulled a corner of one of his trouser patches loose, and he fiddled with it idly.

"Matter of fact, my brother and I were probably going to sleep in here anyway," Chicks said. "Since it's got some straw and all."

"Right . . . and when you consider that we got to eat our fill of oranges," Finn added, "I have to say our lot in life has actually improved somewhat."

"Yep," Dutch agreed.

"Oh . . . okay," Alexander said, sounding relieved. "That's good."

Frances couldn't pretend to ignore all this anymore, and she turned to face Finn and the other older boys. "Are you just saying that to be nice?" she asked. "Because you don't have to be nice to Alexander."

Finn shook his head. "It's all the same to us, I tell you. We were being sent off to work in some wretched factory before we met you. And now we're still being sent off to work in some wretched factory. Only difference is, we got oranges now." He smiled a thin, sad smile.

"Too bad none of us are going to Wanderville," Chicks said. "It sounded real nice."

"But we can still go—" Alexander started to tell him, but Chicks just shook his head.

"Our mama still needs us to work to pay off her debts. Same with Dutch's pa, and Owney's folks."

Frances had nearly forgotten that the boys' families owed money to Edwin Adolphius—or someone who worked for him. *That must be an awful feeling,* she thought. They were all quiet for a moment, and Frances wondered if Alexander was thinking the same thing she was. These boys didn't mind sleeping in filthy straw in a livestock pen. They were a lot worse off than she and Harold and her friends.

Finally Alexander spoke up.

"What if you could just pay those debts?" he asked the older boys. "Instead of having to work them off."

"How?" Dutch muttered. "With what money?"

"Reward money," Alexander said. "Like the money we're going to get at the World's Fair. If we can all escape from this boat, that is."

Frances caught her breath in surprise and saw Jack and Eli turn around, intrigued. It was an interesting idea—all of them working together to escape the steamboat! And if they split the money, it would help these boys. Maybe she was wrong to think Alexander was so selfish.

"Hmm," Finn said, looking at Alexander. "Tell us more."

Jack took out the medallion to show everyone, and Alexander told them all about meeting Zogby and how he'd given them instructions to find a person named Mr. McGee at the World's Fair and deliver it to him for a reward.

Owney grinned. "Sounds easy enough."

"I don't know," Dutch said. "It seems a little fishy. Why do you trust this Zogby fellow? You'd only just met him. What if he's lying?"

Even though Frances hoped the older boys were willing to help them escape, she had to admit she'd had similar worries about Zogby. She still did, in fact.

"Look, if the fellow's lying, we still have the medallion," Jack pointed out. "Which we can sell."

The older boys appeared to think about this for a moment and exchanged looks with one another. Finally Finn said, "Okay, we'll escape with you. But we're still all going to Wanderville, too, right?"

"Of course!" Alexander exclaimed.

"Do you think we could go there first?" Owney asked.

"We're always there!" Harold said.

Owney dismissed him with a wave of his hand and turned back to Alexander. "I know you've gone there a lot, but maybe you could take us there *before* we go to the Fair. If ain't too much trouble, that is."

"Yeah, those hot buttered rolls sound good," Chicks said.

"Sure!" Alexander said, grinning. "It's never too much trouble to go."

"Do you think I could work in that bakery?"

Dutch asked. "You know, the one that sells those rolls. You suppose they pay good wages?"

Alexander nodded and grinned. "You can do whatever you want," he said.

It was then that Frances realized that there was something strange about the conversation Alexander was having with the older boys. She looked over at Jack, who was also listening in, and she could tell by his expression that he knew it, too.

These boys don't know what Wanderville really is, she realized. They still thought it was like other towns—real-life towns. She and Jack could tell by the way the boys talked about it, and by the questions they asked Alexander.

But Alexander couldn't tell.

13
HOCUS-POCUS STUFF

Jack guessed it was pretty late at night, judging from the way the ragtime piano music from the upper decks had given way to slower songs and the din of passenger voices had quieted down.

By now Harold was curled up fast asleep in the straw, and Eli had dozed off as well. Frances had her *Eclectic Third Reader* out and was trying her best to use the meager lamplight outside the animal pen to make out the words. Meanwhile, Alexander and the older boys were still excitedly talking over in the far corner. As for Jack, he had been lying in his corner for a while trying unsuccessfully to sleep. Finally, he crept over to where Frances sat with her book. She seemed grateful to have someone to talk with, too.

"It's too dark to read." Frances sighed. "I've

just been listening to Alexander and the boys talking. They're talking about the World's Fair now, but before that, they were talking about Wanderville, and . . ." She took a deep breath. "And, well, you heard how *that* went. It's clear those boys don't know the truth."

Jack nodded in agreement. "The problem is that Alexander thinks they're just playing along and thinking up new things to build."

"Should we tell them what Wanderville really is?"

"I don't know," Jack said.

"I don't either," Frances whispered. "Maybe not yet. Or not here. It would change everything."

Over in the corner Alexander was smiling from ear to ear as Dutch dealt out playing cards to their group.

"I was so mad at him for not telling us about that conversation between Miss DeHaven and Mr. Adolphius." Jack rubbed his cramped legs and sighed. "But I guess it was just too hard for him to tell us. And now that I see how happy he is, I feel the same way about telling those boys Wanderville isn't what they think it is. It would be too hard."

Frances agreed. "He *is* happier now. And I'm glad he's getting along better with Finn and his gang."

"Also, he's excited about going to the Fair," Jack pointed out. "Remember when he didn't think it was a good idea for us to go?"

Frances's expression suddenly shifted. "Yeah, well . . ."

"What? You're not still suspicious of Mr. Zogby, are you?"

"I'm not the only one who is, Jack. Didn't you hear Dutch say it all seemed kind of fishy?" She turned to the flyleaf of her book where she kept her notes. "All Zogby wrote was a name, 'Mr. C. McGee.' Then as he was driving off he said to look for '*Moses* McGee at the Temple of Promises.' Come on, the *Temple of Promises*? None of it makes any sense! And then there's that medallion thing you've got—"

Jack interrupted. "Look, there's something going on with that medallion, I tell you." He pulled it out of his pocket and held it up in the light. "I didn't have a chance to tell anyone yet, but when we were over by the orange crates I saw something carved into the wood on a trunk over there."

He found the symbols on the medallion—the one that looked like a loop with loose ends, and the one like a letter *M* with an arrow—and pointed them out to Frances. "See these? Somebody scratched those into the wood! I don't know what it means but it can't be coincidence, you know?"

Frances just squinted at him.

Jack sighed—of course she wouldn't understand. *He* didn't understand what the symbols meant either. He simply had a feeling that the medallion had come their way for a reason, and the feeling had gotten stronger once he'd seen the symbols scratched into the trunk. But he couldn't tell Frances any of this. She'd only laugh and say it was all "hocus-pocus stuff."

So instead he said, "Look. I don't care what you think. Going after the reward for the medallion is the only choice we have! It's the only way we can keep Wanderville going and get us money for California."

"Oh, what do *you* care?" Frances sputtered back. "*You're* the one who's planning on going back to New York!"

"I'm *not* planning! That was just an idea!" Jack protested. That wasn't quite true—he really had been thinking a lot lately about going back to New York—but he hadn't decided anything. "Honestly, I don't know what I'm going to do. All I know is that we have to escape *this* place first!"

"Yeah, that's for sure," Frances muttered. She

closed her book and crawled over to sleep near Harold. "Maybe that magic medallion of yours will tell you how. Good-night, Jack."

Frances woke to the sound of the *Addie Dauphin*'s bells clanging. She could glimpse a bit of blue sky and morning daylight over the stacks of cargo that surrounded the pen.

Everyone else was awake by now—though Frances wondered if Alexander and the older boys had even slept, since they were still yammering on, only now Jack and Eli had joined them and they were talking about escape plans.

"What if we jammed something in that big paddle wheel?" Chicks was saying. "Would that stop the boat?"

Oh, brother, Frances thought. She was glad the older boys were going to escape with them, but she wondered if any of them were really smart enough to figure out how. She listened until Harold tugged her sleeve.

"Frannie, my nose isn't leaking anymore!"

Frances smiled and began to pick bits of straw out of her little brother's hair. "The oranges must have helped cure your cold."

"I wish we could have more," Harold whispered. "I'm hungry."

But they hardly needed to wonder about food, because a few minutes later they heard the sound of boots in the corridor outside the pen, and one of the deckhands appeared with a big pot and two wooden spoons.

"The cook saved some mush for you brats," he muttered. He tried to shove the pot between the bars of the pen, but it was too wide. Grumbling complaints under his breath, he unlocked the tall gate, stepped inside, and set the pot down with a *thunk*.

Everyone was silent for a moment.

"Er . . . thank you," Alexander said.

"Two hours 'til we dock in St. Louis," the deckhand told them. "Then we'll come back down and take you to the factory." He tossed out a rag from his pocket. "Make sure you clean that pot real good when you're done with it."

Dutch nodded. "Got it."

"And you're not getting out of this pen until we come get you, you hear? Especially *you*." The deckhand turned to Eli, who was now standing right by the open gate. "I don't trust your kind. You weren't trying to slip out, were you?"

"No, sir!" Eli replied, and he sat back down.

The deckhand pulled the gate shut and locked it with a key he kept on a ring on his belt. Then he stomped off out of sight, the noise of his boots fading away.

The mush—some kind of cornmeal, Frances guessed—was cold and tasteless, but it wasn't hard to eat. The nine of them passed the pot around twice, and while they did, they continued to discuss their escape. From what Frances could tell, the only plans the older boys had come up with involved ways to subdue the deckhand.

"I can trip him," Dutch said. "And then Finn, you can jump on his back and start clobbering him!"

"Shouldn't we start thinking about ways to actually get *off* the boat, too?" Alexander asked.

Owney ignored him. "Frances, maybe you'll have to be the one to clobber Miss DeHaven, since you're a girl."

Frances almost choked. "What? Wait a minute—why do we have to clobber *anyone*?" She tried to imagine winding her arm up and punching Miss DeHaven in the nose. Fine—so it was fun to *imagine*, but it was another thing to *do* it.

"Well, do *you* all have any other ideas?" Finn asked, looking at Frances and her friends.

Everyone fell silent. Then Eli, who hadn't said anything for quite a while, spoke up.

"I've got a lot of ideas. But first, we've got to get out of this pen," he said.

Dutch laughed. "No kidding. But how?"

Eli got up and went over to the gate. He knelt down and peered into the lock, then took a long piece of straw and threaded one end through the keyhole. He reached through the bars around to the other side of the lock and grabbed the straw end where it came out.

"You can't pick a lock with straw," Finn whispered. "Can you?"

Eli motioned for everyone to come over for a closer look. "One of the sheds at the Carey farm had a lock like this and I learned how to keep it from sticking." He pointed to the little slot along the edge of the gate where the latch was supposed to fit. It was packed with straw. "See that straw? I stuffed it in there when the deckhand fellow brought us breakfast. Now I can pull the latch back even more with a strong piece of straw."

Eli had both ends of the straw now, one in each hand, and he yanked it back and forth, hard, until it seemed to catch on something.

"Almost got it," he said. "Now someone's just got to try the handle."

Frances stepped forward. Holding her breath, she turned the handle just above the gate lock. To her surprise, it gave way with a soft *click*!

"I think it's unlocking!" she said with a gasp. And then, in one easy motion, she pulled open the gate.

14
OPERATION HUCKLEBERRY

*L*isten *for the whistle. Then count to a hundred.*

Jack kept repeating the directions in his head as he waited in the luggage hold with Eli. The escape plan Eli had come up with was a good one, but it involved an awful lot of waiting.

Right now, on the upper deck, Frances and Harold were doing some waiting of their own. They too wouldn't move until they heard the whistle. Once it sounded, Frances would distract the first-class passengers with her dancing—one of the Irish jigs she used to perform for coins down on the Bowery.

Meanwhile, in the livestock pen, Alexander, Finn, and Chicks were waiting for the right moment to create a noisy diversion for the deckhands, and over by the bow, Dutch and Owney were getting ready to put out the gangplank.

The patch of sky Jack could see from his hiding spot was getting hazier, the kind of haze that came from a city's chimneys and smokestacks. They had to be close to docking. That was when the *Addie Dauphin*'s whistle would sound, just as the boat was about to arrive in St. Louis. Jack tried not to think about the fact that Edwin Adolphius's canning factory was nearby.

"Do you think we missed the whistle?" he whispered to Eli.

Eli shook his head. "Not a chance. That thing is right over our heads. And if the plan wasn't going right, we'd know." They had all agreed that if something went wrong, the code word to shout was *huckleberry,* and so far nobody had shouted it. "Just calm down."

Jack breathed out. "Aren't *you* nervous?"

Eli grinned. "Well, I keep thinking there's someone looking over our shoulder, and *that* feels funny."

Jack turned and looked back at the straw-stuffed figure wearing a red flannel shirt, brown trousers, and a black derby hat. "Well, at least he's on *our* side."

They'd discovered the shirt and trousers and hat in one of the heavier trunks. The figure's head was a lady's stocking stuffed with cotton from the cargo bales, and its feet were socks packed with straw. They'd even found a pair of shoes, but everyone realized that Owney could use them more. In the end they had something that was a lot like a scarecrow, only better, because it was going to do much more than stand on a post in a cornfield.

"We should call him O'Reilly," Eli said. O'Reilly was the mean farmhand who'd bossed him around back at the Careys' place. "What do you think?"

Jack laughed and was just about to answer when the whistle began to sound. It gave off a long, low call that everyone on the boat could hear.

"Finally!" Eli said under his breath. "Start counting!"

Jack nodded. *Four five six seven eight nine ten eleven* . . . He was trying not to count too fast.

He and Eli each took an arm of the dummy. "Come on, O'Reilly, let's get a move on," Jack muttered as they began to drag it toward the railing. *Thirty-two thirty-three thirty-four thirty-five* . . . Now they had only a minute.

"Wait a second!" Jack cried as soon as they got

to the railing. "His arm came loose!" He reached up inside the dummy's shirtsleeve and tried to pack the straw more tightly.

Just then Dutch and Owney came running back from the bow.

"We got the gangplank ready!" Dutch cried. "But . . . uh . . ." He gasped and shook his head.

"What is it?" Jack asked.

"*Huckleberry!*" Owney shouted. "You've got to hurry! Finn found something real strange under the cotton bales and we might be in even bigger trouble if we don't hustle."

Jack could hear boots pounding the deck in the direction Owney and Dutch had come from. Someone was after them—getting closer—but still out of sight for the moment. He and Eli exchanged a panicked look. They couldn't let anyone see them doing what they were about to do.

With only seconds to spare, they lifted O'Reilly as high as they could over the railing, swung back, and let go.

On the upper deck, Harold was counting. "Sixty-five sixty-six sixty-seven sixty-eight . . ."

"Shh! Quit counting out loud!" Frances hissed.

She was trying to focus on her dance steps and match her rhythm to the jaunty piano music coming from the nearby parlor. She felt self-conscious enough in the dress she'd borrowed from one of the trunks in the luggage hold. The dress was lacy and yellow, and she had pulled it on over her breeches and shirt in the little hidden stairwell between decks. She hoped to be rid of it by the time they were all off the boat, because if Dutch or Finn saw her in this getup they'd laugh their heads off, and Alexander would give her a funny look, too. Good thing they were all elsewhere at the moment.

Point foot, then bring it back. Step left, step front, hop . . . Frances tried to concentrate more on her footwork than on the faces of the passengers who were now stopping to watch her. Her job was to make sure they were paying attention to *her,* instead of what was about to happen on the other side of the boat.

Turn, bring foot back, step right, step front . . . She made sure she was wearing her brightest smile. A couple of older women nodded kindly as they watched her. There were half a dozen passengers in her audience now, and Frances wondered if it would be enough. . . .

Just then came the deckhand's cry. "MAN OVERBOARD!"

Already? Frances thought.

A murmur went up among the passengers who had been watching Frances dance. She stopped mid-jig and looked over at Harold, who was still counting to himself, only now silently. *Eighty-five, eighty-six,* he stood and mouthed, but his eyes were wide with surprise.

Frances grabbed his arm. "Come on!" Everyone around them was rushing over to the other side of the boat to watch the rescue, but she and Harold headed straight for the large stairway that led to the lowest deck.

From the top of the stairs Frances could see that the boat had reached the dock and the gangway ramp was in place. All they had to do was run down those stairs and in a few more steps they'd be free! But then someone stepped right in front of her and Harold. A steward in a blue and gold uniform.

"Miss, it's not time to go ashore yet," he said, blocking their way.

"But—but we're at the dock," Frances protested.

"Miss, you'll have to wait until the situation down on the main deck has been resolved." He lowered his voice and whispered confidentially, "That's no 'man overboard'—just a dummy stuffed with straw. Some kind of prank!"

"Oh!" Frances tried to sound surprised. "You don't say!"

"They're trying to catch the brats responsible right now," the steward replied. "They're all—" He stopped suddenly and grabbed at the air. "What's this?"

"It's snowing!" Harold laughed.

Before Frances could ask what on earth he meant, she saw a tuft of something white and fluffy float by on the breeze, and then another tuft, and another.

"Is that . . . *cotton*?" the steward said incredulously.

It *was* cotton, Frances realized. Cotton from the bales down on the lowest deck, scattering in the wind.

Harold ran over to the railing that overlooked the lowest deck. "Look!" he cried, and Frances followed.

Down on the front deck where the big cargo was kept, Finn and Chicks and Alexander were running among the stacks of cotton bales, tearing them apart. There was now a dazzling blizzard of drifting cotton bits, and three of the deckhands were in the midst of it all, swatting at the deluge. But instead of trying to stop the boys, they were busy grabbing big wooden casks and stowing them out of sight in another cargo hold.

Frances blinked. Where had those barrels come from?

"See, Frannie?" Harold said. "I knew there was something hidden under those bales when I jumped on one of them!"

Frances leaned over for a better look. There were words stamped on the barrels—MADEIRA RUM AND RYE WHISKEY. She sucked in her breath. She had a feeling those casks weren't supposed to be on a boat like this—and that was why they'd been covered up. Now that the boys had discovered the casks were there, uncovering them was a perfect distraction to keep the deckhands busy!

Harold pointed down to the deck again. "Here come Dutch and Owney! And Jack and Eli, too!" The boys were making their way through the maze of cargo, heading toward the bow and the gangplank that led from the lower deck to the dock.

Alexander looked up and spotted Frances and Harold. He began to wave frantically. *Come on!* he mouthed as Finn and Chicks ran past him and joined the others in the cargo stacks.

Frances's heart began to pound. "They're all about to go ashore!" she whispered to Harold. "But we're still stuck up here!" She glanced over to the large stairway, which was still being guarded by the steward, along with another uniformed member of the crew. "What do we do now?"

Harold chewed his lip and got on his tiptoes to peer over the railing. "I know!" he cried. He clambered over the deck railing and hung on to the other side. "We'll climb down!"

"Harold!" Frances hissed. "No! It's too dangerous."

"You know how good I can climb, Frannie. So can you!"

Frances scanned the upper deck. Maybe there was another set of stairs somewhere, but it would cost her and Harold precious seconds to find them. But here they had a clear view of the way off the boat, and they were right above the spot where they needed to be. About ten or twelve feet above, she guessed. Too high to jump, but . . .

"Okay," Frances muttered. She yanked the yellow dress over her head—silly thing—and tossed it aside, glad to be back in her boys' breeches. Then she swung one leg over the side of the railing. It was just like climbing down from a fire escape, she tried to tell herself. Except *backward* . . .

15

A CLOSE CALL

Jack turned in all directions. "Where are Frances and Harold?!"

"Keep your head down!" Eli called in a loud whisper. "We're not off this boat yet!"

They were close enough to the gangplank to make a run for it, but Eli had suddenly ducked down next to a stack of crates and motioned for Jack to get down, too.

"One of the deckhands was getting awfully close," he explained. "But I don't think he saw us. . . . Hey, what's this?"

He was peering into the open end of one of the crates. Jack had noticed, too, the way something inside was oddly shiny and caught the light. Eli reached over and pulled out a small, flat bottle with a crudely printed label that said PURE GIN.

"I bet *this* smells foul," Eli said, but before he could say more, they heard footsteps. Jack crouched down even lower as two of the burliest deckhands passed by.

"Here's the bottled stuff!" one of them said, thumping a crate right near Jack. "Boss says to stow these back in the luggage hold!"

"What about the river rats?" the other asked, and Jack felt a prickle down his spine. They were talking about him and his friends!

"Get 'em if you can, but Boss says hide all the booze first now that it's been uncovered. Besides, he says he knows where to look for those runts if they go ashore."

"Heh-heh, what kid *wouldn't* want to see that fair." The first one chuckled as they grabbed a few of the crates and stomped off.

"Uh-oh," Jack muttered as he and Eli stood up again.

"Uh-oh is right," said Eli, pointing up. "There are Frances and Harold!"

Jack turned to see Frances shimmying down one

of the support posts that held up the upper deck balcony. But Harold stayed where he was, clinging to the woodwork beneath the upper deck rail, and Jack realized he'd gotten his foot caught.

Frances let herself drop the last few feet and landed in a crouch. The two boys rushed over, joined by Alexander and the older boys.

"Harold . . ." she panted. "Stuck!"

"My hands are all hot!" Harold whimpered above them, one foot swinging free.

"I know!" Jack called. "But don't let go."

The spot where Harold clung was closer to the upper deck than the lower, and for a moment it seemed that all he needed to do was climb back to where he started. But then a fellow in a fancy uniform leaned out over the railing and glared down at all of them.

"Don't go back up, Harold!" Frances fretted. "You'll get caught!"

"But it's hard to hold on!" he cried. His arms started to shake.

Just then Alexander seized the support post and began to pull himself up to meet Harold. He reached out and grabbed the younger boy's belt in the back. "It's all right. I've got you!" he said.

"And we've got you, too!" Dutch called. He and the other three older boys were standing with their arms held out and clasped tightly together to make a sort of safety net.

"Nothing to be afraid of, Harold!" Jack said, and he believed it, too. They were all working together, all nine of them. They all wanted the same thing—to get off this boat, to be on their own.

Harold stopped shaking. He took a deep breath, found a foothold with his free foot, and then suddenly yanked his stuck foot loose.

"I'm free!" he yelled, and clambered over to the support pole, where he slid down right after Alexander.

"Now let's *go*!" Finn shouted, heading for the gangplank.

His brother was right behind him. "To Wanderville!" Chicks called.

Jack had never thought he could move so fast across something as narrow as the gangplank. But his scurrying feet took him to the soft boards of the dock at last. They were on shore!

"We did it!" Eli shouted. Both boys stopped to catch their breath.

Behind them, Frances and Harold had just leapt off the gangplank and were running to catch up. And just ahead, Alexander and the older boys thumped one another on the back and cheered. Jack and Eli started to walk over to join them, but after a few steps, Jack paused.

"What is it?" Eli asked.

"Dutch and his friends want to go to Wanderville," Jack said. "But they don't know what it is."

He couldn't hear what Alexander was saying to the older boys, but they weren't cheering anymore. Their faces were now serious.

Frances and Harold caught up with Jack and Eli. "What's going on?" Frances asked Jack. She looked over to the group of boys. "What are they talking about?"

"They're learning the truth about Wanderville," Jack said.

Frances sucked in her breath. "Uh-oh."

They could see that Dutch's eyes had narrowed, and Owney had crossed his arms. Alexander was still grinning, but he was looking from one face to another anxiously.

Jack and Frances drew closer to listen in.

"You better give us a straight answer," Chicks threatened.

Finn glared at Alexander. "I'm asking you again," he said. "Where's *Wanderville*?"

"I told you!" Alexander replied. "It's always been here! Or wherever you want it to be!"

Jack's mouth went dry and he turned to Frances. She looked stricken, and he knew she realized the same thing he did. *They think Alexander is playing a trick on them!*

"You told us you were going to *take* us there," Dutch muttered. "And it ain't here, is it?"

"That's not true!" Alexander protested. "It's just that—"

"So you're saying *we're* the liars?" Owney interrupted. "You're trying to play us for fools, aren't you?" He turned to Finn. "I *told* you he was trying to put something over on us."

"No! I'm not! It's just . . . Wanderville isn't . . ."

"Isn't *real*?" Dutch shot back.

Alexander went pale just then. He opened his mouth to say something, but then just turned and started running down the dock toward the boatyard.

"Wait!" Frances called. She grabbed Harold's hand and they set out after Alexander.

The older boys, though, stayed where they were. Owney muttered something about Alexander being a "shifty-eyed worm," but Jack was relieved that they weren't going to beat up Alexander.

Instead, though, they suddenly turned and went straight toward Jack and Eli, their faces grim and determined.

"Wait a second," Jack said, backing up, his hands out in front of him. "We can explain!"

Dutch just shook his head. Finn and Chicks grabbed Jack's arms and pinned them behind his back, while Owney guarded Eli. Then Dutch reached out and yanked Jack by his shirt collar.

"Look, your friend Alexander's got some strange ideas, that's for sure. As far as we can tell, there's only one thing he's told us about that's real, and *you've* got it!"

Jack felt a lurch in his stomach as he realized what Dutch meant. *The medallion!* Dutch immediately began rifling through Jack's pockets.

"No, wait!" Jack protested. "You can't take—"

But Dutch had found the medallion and was holding it up with a grin. "Sorry to have to do this," he said. "But we got ourselves into a lot of trouble on that boat on account of you guys, you and your crazy stories about some town that don't even exist!"

"Yeah, you owe us," Finn added.

"And getting that reward's the only thing that'll make it right," Chicks put in.

"I still think the whole scheme sounds fishy," Dutch said. "But not as fishy as the other stuff you and your friends told us." He pocketed the medallion.

Finn and Chicks dropped Jack's arms and pushed him to the ground, while Owney gave Eli a rough shove.

"Thanks for everything," Dutch said with a sneer. "We'll think of you kindly at the World's Fair!"

Then the older boys took off running toward the shipyard, turned a corner, and were out of sight.

16
CLANG, CLANG, CLANG!

"I knew that medallion thing was bad luck!" Eli muttered as they ran.

"It's not!" Jack insisted, between breaths. "We've got to get it back!"

The five of them were racing down alleyways and narrow streets among the vast riverfront warehouses, dim passages that smelled of hot tar and sometimes fish. Frances kept looking over her shoulder expecting to see someone from the *Addie Dauphin* running after them, but as far as she could tell, they weren't being followed.

Instead, *they* were the ones doing the chasing. Frances wished she'd been close enough to do something—*say* something—when she'd seen Dutch and his gang shake down Jack for the medallion. She still didn't think there was anything special about that crazy piece of junk, but she hated that those boys were being bullies, especially Finn and Chicks. Frances knew that Jack wanted to get the medallion back, but more than anything she wanted to catch those louts so she could yell her head off at them.

Just then the five of them reached the end of the alley where it met with a wide street that bustled with traffic. They were getting closer to downtown St. Louis! They stopped to catch their breath.

It felt strange to be in a city again, with the sky chopped up into the little strips between buildings. That used to be the only way Frances would see her days, and she'd had no idea it could be so different.

"Which way do we go?" Alexander panted.

"And where's the Fair?" Harold asked.

"I think I just saw them!" Jack cried. "Across the street!"

Sure enough, there were Dutch and Owney and Finn and Chicks, striding along two by two, talking among themselves. Frances glared at them. *Those rats!*

As if they could sense her glare, Finn glanced across the street, and then so did the other boys. When they saw Frances and her friends, they took off running.

Jack was the first one to dart out into the street after them.

"Watch out!" Eli yelled as a milk truck missed hitting them so narrowly that it made the horses rear up.

They wove their way through the stream of buggies and trucks and motorcars as fast as they could, until suddenly—*Clang! Clang!*—the bells of an approaching trolley warned them.

"It's been a while since I had to stay out of the way of one of these things," Jack remarked as they jumped clear of the tracks in the street.

It took only a moment or two for the trolley to go by. Then they sprinted the last few yards to the other side of the street.

But the boys were gone.

Frances whirled around. "They caught the streetcar!"

The trolley was more than a block away by now, but she could still make out the figures of four boys clinging to the iron stairs in the back of the car.

"*Blast it!*" she spat, not even caring that Harold would hear her swear.

Jack was looking at a placard attached to a

lamppost. "This sign says this line goes to the Fair. All we have to do is catch the next one!"

They found a corner where the trolley would stop. Frances couldn't stand the wait, so she crouched down to check the buttons on her little brother's shoes.

"Why didn't Finn and Dutch and the rest of them want to stay with us?" Harold asked. "I thought they were going to become citizens of Wanderville."

Frances sighed and looked over at Alexander, who was standing nearby with his hands deep in his pockets, staring down at the bricks of the street. "They didn't understand what Wanderville was," she said.

"I should have explained it to them better," Alexander added softly.

But what if they understood and still *didn't want to be citizens?* Frances wondered. She was glad when the next trolley appeared after a few minutes and she didn't have to think about it anymore.

They climbed aboard and Alexander paid the fare for all of them from the money Zogby had given them.

"I wish we didn't have to spend this money,"

Frances whispered as they found long wooden benches to sit on. "I bet Dutch and his friends managed to hitch a ride on their car without paying."

"We can't risk getting in trouble now," Alexander pointed out. "Not when we just escaped. And speaking of that, we still have the steamboat fare money that we didn't spend."

"It's not enough," Jack muttered.

"Not enough for what?" Frances asked.

Jack didn't answer. But just then the view outside the trolley changed, with the brick row houses giving way to a vast park, and in the distance—just a mile or two away—the domes and spires of what appeared to be an enchanted city. They all stood to get a better view.

"It's the Fair, isn't it?" Eli said.

"Look at the wheel!" Harold whispered. "It's huge!"

There it was, the famous Ferris wheel, looking exactly like the etching Frances had seen once in an old newspaper. She had heard some of the upper-deck passengers on the *Addie Dauphin* talking about how it had been built in Chicago years ago and then rebuilt here for the Fair. Now the wheel turned slowly, stopping every so often and then starting again, quiet and graceful in the distance. It looked almost magic, Frances thought. Like you could look at it and make a wish.

As the trolley sped closer to the Fair the buildings began to appear even more jewel-like, and just beyond them lay the shining surface of a lagoon. It was all far more grand than Coney Island, Frances realized.

"It's so . . . big," Jack said, and from the tone of his voice, Frances could tell what he was thinking: How were they ever going to find the older boys in a place as big as the St. Louis World's Fair, much less the person who was supposed to get the medallion?

They were still dumbstruck when the trolley came to a terminal and slowed to stop.

"End of the line!" the conductor called. "The Louisiana Purchase Exposition!"

Frances grabbed Harold's hand as the five of them stepped down from the trolley steps and walked into a bright, bustling plaza outside the Fair's front gate. The sun was high overhead and Frances counted nearly a dozen black parasols being carried by fairgoers. There was no sign of Dutch or Finn or the other older boys, though Frances had a feeling that they couldn't be far.

"Look!" Harold cried. "A mountain! Right over there!"

They all looked where Harold pointed. Just to the right of the front gates was a mountain—a very fake one, craggy and with fake snow—looming over a boundary wall. "I want to look!" he said, and he dropped Frances's hand and ran over to the wall for a closer look. Frances and the others followed.

"That's not a real mountain, you know," Frances said, even though she secretly thought it was impressive.

Alexander agreed. "And look, Harold. Real mountains don't have doors on the side of them." He motioned over to a steel door in the wall, partially hidden by hedges, that said TYROLEAN ALPS—EMPLOYEES ONLY.

"I wonder if it opens!" Harold said, running over to the door.

"Harold, no!" Frances said. She started to go after him but suddenly felt a sharp pull on the back of her collar.

"As a matter of fact, Queenie, it *does* open," said a voice.

Finn!

"Let me go, you snake!" Frances yanked herself

free, then whirled around to see that Dutch had Alexander by the collar, and Chicks and Owney had Jack and Eli.

"So good to see you all again!" Dutch said.

Harold stood with his hand on the doorknob, his mouth open in shock.

"You can open that door, Harold," Dutch said. "And let's all go inside, shall we? We got business to discuss in private."

17
A DEAL IS STRUCK

The door in the mountain led to a stuffy passageway lit by an electric bulb. Once they were all inside, Chicks shut the door.

Jack braced himself, ready to fight, but Chicks had let go of his collar, and no one else was being restrained.

"You'd think it would be more exciting inside the Tyrolean Alps," Finn remarked, motioning around him. "But it ain't."

"Can't even sneak into the Fair this way," Dutch grumbled. "We already tried." He pointed to a ladder that stretched up into darkness. "That thing just leads up to a little door at the top of the mountain. So then you're inside the fairgrounds but you can't go nowheres except down the ladder again, because it's too steep to get down the outside of that mountain without breaking your neck."

"What's your point?" Jack said.

Dutch reached into his pocket and pulled out the medallion. He handed it to Finn, who was tall enough to hold it up out of everyone else's reach. "Maybe we were wrong to throw you over and try to get the reward ourselves," he told Jack and his friends.

"Oh, really?" Frances folded her arms.

"Well, have you seen the Fair?" Owney said. "It's huge!"

Finn swung the medallion. "We suspect you might know more about where to deliver this thing."

Alexander's face brightened a bit. "So, you still want to split the reward with us, if we tell you what we know?"

But Dutch only glowered. "Here's the thing. We don't trust a word you little weasels say. You haven't exactly been truthful about this Wanderville business. We weren't even sure if you were telling the truth about this medallion!"

"We are, we swear," Jack said. He wanted so badly to just jump up and snatch the medallion out of Finn's hand.

Chicks shook his head. "The only reason we know that it's worth anything is because you followed us to get it back."

"Look," Alexander said. "I'm sorry if we gave you the wrong idea about Wanderville. But we all can still help each other."

Dutch and Finn exchanged glances. "Maybe we'll *make* you tell us how to deliver the medallion and collect the reward," Dutch said.

"Or maybe you'll just have to trust us!" Frances said. She went over and pulled Harold closer. "*We* trusted *you* when we were escaping from the steamboat. Remember when Harold almost fell and you said you would catch him? We believed you!" Harold nodded at that. "And now you need to believe us."

Jack held his breath and kept his eyes on the medallion and its shiny carvings. The wings of the bird glinted in the dim light of the passageway, and he stared hard at the strange symbols. There were so many reasons why he wanted the medallion back again, but one of the biggest ones, for sure, was to find out what those symbols meant.

Dutch was silent for a moment. Then he motioned to Finn, who finally lowered his arm and held out the medallion.

"All right," Dutch said. "We're a team again."

Jack grabbed the medallion and felt a strange surge of relief as he closed his fingers around its edges.

Eli spoke up. "There's just one thing," he said. "What about Edwin Adolphius and Miss DeHaven? They're going to be looking for us. And they know we were heading here to the Fair. Jack and I heard the deckhands say so."

Jack suddenly remembered what the deckhand had said: *What kid wouldn't want to see that fair?*

"Good point," Owney said. "But that's where we can help. Because we've been thinking . . ." He looked over at the ladder. "The top of this here mountain is a great lookout."

"It sure is," Finn added. "We can see everyone who comes through that front gate, and a lot of the fairgrounds, too. If Miss DeHaven and Edwin Adolphius come here after us, we'll spot 'em."

"But if we're at the Fair," Frances said, "and you're up there, how will you warn us that they're coming?"

"We could whistle," Chicks said. "I can whistle real good!"

Finn laughed. "Naw. You might be able to call

home our hound dogs from the woods, but no way any whistle, even yours, can carry over all that noise and ruckus out there."

"Wait, I got it!" Dutch said. "We'll fly a flag up there!"

Owney pulled a red bandana out of his pocket. "We can tie this to a stick and put it out if we see Adolphius."

"That's perfect!" Frances said. "Besides, they'll be looking for nine kids together, so if you fellows are on lookout, there will be fewer of us walking around the fairgrounds." She turned to Jack. "Don't you think that's a good plan?"

"Uh, sure," Truthfully, Jack didn't like the idea of splitting up. He always worried that someone would be left behind, the way Quentin and the other kids at the Pratcherds' had been. Or the way he and Daniel had gotten separated in the fire back in New York. It didn't matter whether Dutch and Finn and Owney and Chicks were his friends—all he knew was that they needed to be free. And the reward money from the medallion would do them some good. Jack would be able to help them, and he figured their luck could only get better once he went back to New York.

"We could take turns on lookout duty," Alexander suggested.

"Nope," Dutch replied. "Me and my gang don't mind keeping an eye on things. Make sure no funny business happens." He gave Jack and Alexander and Eli a pointed look. Jack was sure that by "keeping an eye on things" Dutch meant keeping an eye on *them*.

"Suit yourself," Jack told Dutch. He tucked the medallion back into his pocket.

"But we'll come back with the reward no matter what," Frances put in.

"We promise," Alexander added.

Then one by one, Jack, Eli, Frances, Harold, and Alexander slipped out the door in the wall beneath the mountain and went back to the plaza outside the entrance gates. From their hiding spot, the older boys nodded as if to say *good luck*. Then they shut the door.

"I bet they're going up to the lookout now," Frances said, squinting up at the peak of the big fake mountain.

Jack squinted as he looked up, too. They couldn't see much from the ground, but after a few minutes, they could just make out a hand waving back at them from behind a crag near the peak.

Alexander nodded at Jack. "There's no turning back now."

Jack patted the pocket where he kept the medallion.

"That's for certain." He turned to grin at Frances and Harold and Eli. "Guess we have no choice but to go to the World's Fair."

And, with that, they headed straight for the turnstiles.

18
SEARCHING FOR THE TEMPLE OF PROMISES

Frances swore the Louisiana Purchase Monument was as tall as any building on Broadway. It was this *thing* with stone cherubs all over it, and wreaths, and eagles, and a statue of Thomas Jefferson, and there was a big shiny globe with a statue of a cheering fellow perched on top like a trophy. It was the first grand sight of the Fair when one walked in through the front gates. Or that's what Frances thought at first, until she saw the shining water of the Grand Basin, and then the giant domed palace across the water.

I don't know what to look at first! she thought. The others walked next to her silently, and Frances could tell they were as awestruck as she was.

"What's the lou-weezy . . . the Louisiana Purchase?" Harold asked.

"It's the . . . it's . . ." Frances was so distracted by the splendor all around them that she had to scrunch her eyes shut to remember what she'd learned in school. "It's when Thomas Jefferson bought the Louisiana Territory from France. It's the hundred-year anniversary!"

Harold pointed to a sculpture of a woman wearing nothing but some drapes. "Who's that lady? Is she from France?"

"Sure," Alexander murmured. "Whatever you say."

Frances had to hold back a laugh. Alexander looked like he was in a trance, he was so transfixed by the scenery. It seemed that in every direction there was a spectacular palace adorned with sculptures and tall columns, and that there were flags flying from every soaring rooftop. . . .

"Wait!" Frances stopped in her tracks and turned around, scanning the skyline for the fake mountain peak. Finally she found it, looking just as it had been a half hour ago.

"The signal flag isn't up," Jack said. "Don't worry, Miss DeHaven isn't here!"

"I know," Frances said. "I just don't want to forget to watch for it!" There was so much going on all around them—for example the miniature trains that wound through the fairgrounds, the boats shaped like giant swans gliding around the lagoon—that she knew she could forget plenty of things.

"You know what else we should watch for?" Alexander said. "Food!"

"You're right," Eli said, looking all around. "Something smells good."

Frances noticed the stands and wagons that dotted the parkways as well, and her stomach began to growl as she read the painted signs. There were peanuts for sale, and pastries, frankfurter sandwiches, popcorn, waffles, bottles of something called "Dr Pepper," pecans . . .

"Bananas!" Harold shouted. "They have bananas here!" Harold had never had one before.

Jack, though, seemed anxious. "Look, we can't just spend money all over the place."

"We've got more than you think," Alexander said. "Mr. Zogby gave us fifty cents each for admission to the Fair. But he didn't realize that for kids, it's only *twenty-five* cents to get in! So we have some left over."

"Oh! Well, in that case," Frances said, trying her hardest to sound stern and sensible. "Harold, you may have a banana. It's good for you. And maybe I'll have a small bite of something as well."

"Mrrpfhuff?" Frances said a few minutes later. Her mouth was stuffed so full of honey corn that she couldn't even talk. Jack thought she looked like a squirrel hoarding nuts.

"I *said*, can I see the note that Zogby wrote in your book?" Jack repeated.

"Urff," Frances mumbled, nodding, and stopped to fish her *Third Eclectic Reader* out of her pocket.

They were wandering aimlessly around the lagoon bridges with their hands and pockets stuffed with popped corn and pastries. Jack had too much on his mind to enjoy the food, though. He was trying to remember everything he could about the man that Zogby had told them to find. *Moses McGee, at the Temple of Promises.*

Frances handed Jack her book, and he turned to the flyleaf corner to stare at the name Zogby had written in a quick, flourishing script: *Mr. C. McGee.*

"What I don't get is why he wrote *C.* McGee,"

Jack said, "when a moment later he said the fellow's name was *Moses*."

"Never mind his name," Alexander said. "We just have to find the Temple of Promises, right?"

"Right," Jack said. They'd already asked the banana peddler and the fellow at the popcorn cart about the place, but they'd never heard of it.

"Maybe there's only palaces in this part of the Fair," Eli suggested. "And there's another section with temples." So far, every building they'd seen was a *palace* of some kind—they were just now walking past an enormous place called the Palace of Varied Industries, and across the way was a Palace of Machinery.

"Well, we'll find it," Jack muttered. As far as he was concerned, the sooner they found Mr. McGee, the better. Then they'd have the reward money. And then—Jack wouldn't say this to anyone, of course—then Jack could go. He'd go back to New York, and of course he'd wonder about them, Eli and Alexander and Frances and Harold, but they'd be better off without him, and if he left them the reward money, that would also help, wouldn't it? They could go to California.

"I found this!" Harold cried, handing Jack a slightly crumpled booklet. "It was under that bench. It has a map!"

Daily Official Program, the booklet's cover said. Jack turned to the map page, and Alexander and Frances peered over his shoulder.

"There have to be a hundred buildings here at least," Alexander said. "And some of them aren't even listed on the map."

"Wait!" Frances said, "Down here!" She pointed to the list of buildings at the bottom of the page. "It says Temple . . . Temple of something."

Jack squinted down at the type. "It says 'Temple of Mirth'!"

They all looked up from the map and then at one another.

Eli shrugged. "That's the closest we've gotten so far. Let's go!"

The Temple of Mirth was along a long avenue labeled THE PIKE on the map.

Frances could tell right away that The Pike was different from the rest of the Fair, with its grand plazas and stately places. The crowd was more boisterous, the signs gaudier: NICKELODEON and BEER GARDEN and DANCE HALL.

"Oh!" she gasped. "These are the amusements! Like the boardwalk at Coney Island!"

"This is really something else," Eli said, craning his neck to stare at it all.

The whole street looked like it was trying to be fifty different places all at once—a stone fortress, a model of Ancient Rome, a place called "Paris," and even a ship, all shoved up next to one another. Frances kept her hand on Harold's collar. She knew how anything could distract him, and if he stopped for just a moment in this crowd they could lose track of him.

"Here it is," Jack called from just a few paces ahead. "The Temple of Mirth!"

Frances felt Harold's shoulders stiffen, the way they did when he was scared.

Over the front entrance of the Temple of Mirth was a giant, sculpted face. A *clown* face—staring like an awful painted mask, with a grinning mouth and weird, arched eyebrows.

"Harold, it's just a fun house," Frances told him. "You like those."

"I don't like that clown. His nose has big nostrils."

"There's nothing to be scared of," Frances told Harold. Then she turned to listen to Jack and Alexander talking to the bored-looking fellow in the admission booth.

"Could you please tell us where we can find Moses McGee?" Jack asked him.

"Admission is ten cents," the man muttered.

"But could you just tell us where Mr. McGee is?" Alexander asked. "Is he inside?"

"If he was, you'd still have to pay ten cents." The bored young man picked at a button on the cuff of his shirt.

"So he's inside?" Jack asked.

"I didn't *say* that," the bored man replied. But then something caught his eye behind Frances. "Hey!" he yelled. "You can't just run inside, kid!"

Instinctively Frances turned back to check on Harold. He was gone!

"That little redhead kid just ran inside the fun house!" the man snapped. "He has to pay ten cents!"

"Look, I'll go get him," Frances explained.

The man leaned out of his booth and looked Frances up and down. "You've got a lot of nerve, going around dressed like *that*," he said.

The last thing Frances wanted to discuss right now was her boys' clothes. "Sir, I'll just go inside and fetch my brother—"

Just then Alexander stepped up alongside her. "How she dresses is none of your business!" he said to the man indignantly.

Now Frances felt even more self-conscious with Alexander coming to her defense. Were her silly *pants* going to cause a scene while Harold was getting himself into trouble inside the fun house? "Never mind!" she muttered, and darted inside.

"And *you* have to pay ten cents. . . ." Frances heard the man call after her.

"Harold!" Frances called. "What are you *doing*?"

After a moment, Alexander joined her, followed by Jack and Eli.

"That's *fifty cents* you all owe me!" the man at the front yelled.

The four of them made their way down a dark corridor until they came to a doorway. Frances started to go in, but suddenly a figure appeared right in front of her and she leapt back. "Yikes!"

But the figure was her own reflection. And behind her, Jack's reflection.

"It's a mirror," Jack said. "A maze of mirrors!"

They all began to walk slowly through the maze. "Harold!" Frances called again. She spotted him once, though the mirrors made it look like there were *four* Harolds.

"Ow!" Alexander called. "I just bumped into another mirror that I thought was a doorway!"

"I know! This place is making me seasick!" Eli said.

"I'm over here, Frannie," Harold called. Frances followed his voice until she finally found him near the end of the maze. Then, one by one, the three boys joined them.

"I'm sorry!" Harold cried. "I wanted to get away from the clown!"

"I know, but you're getting us all into trouble!" Frances told him.

"We have to get out of here somehow," Jack insisted. "We didn't pay admission, and if the Fair guards catch us we'll likely get kicked out of the Fair! Then we'll never find Moses McGee."

Alexander snapped his fingers. "I think I saw a door out of here! One of the mirrors had a doorknob in it, right at the height where a doorknob should be. It's just a little ways back there. . . . I mean, *I think*. It's hard to tell in a place like this."

"What if we close our eyes and just feel along the wall?" Jack suggested. "That way our eyes won't trick us."

"Good idea!" Frances said. "But we have to be fast." She could hear voices coming from the direction of the entrance (or what she *thought* was the direction of the entrance, at least).

"I'll lead," Alexander said. He squinted his eyes shut and went step by step sideways down the corridor, keeping his hands along the mirrored wall. Eli followed, then Jack, Harold, and Frances.

"I found the door!" she heard Alexander say, and when she opened her eyes, there it was—a door standing ajar, with daylight coming through!

When Frances made it outside with Harold and the others, they were in a sort of narrow alleyway along the side of the Temple of Mirth.

"Close that door!" Jack said. "Quick, before someone sees!"

But just then Frances felt a hand on her shoulder, and she heard a woman's voice from right behind her.

"It is too late," the voice said. "I have already seen."

19
MADAME ZEE

"All of you," said the woman. "Come with me. *Quick.*"

The woman's face held no expression. She was older and looked stern, with dark hair pulled back tightly and a sharp chin. Her clothes were plain, and she had a badge pinned to her shirtwaist that said OFFICIAL CONCESSIONS—LOUISIANA PURCHASE EXPOSITION.

She led them to the back end of the alley and then down another back-street that appeared to run behind all the buildings on the Pike.

"What's going on?" Jack asked, but really, he knew: They'd been caught.

"You are in trouble," the woman said. "So

you come with me. You hurry." Her voice was all business.

We're sunk! Jack thought. He glanced over at Frances and Alexander and Eli, and could see their faces were grim, too.

They passed street sweepers emptying their sacks of trash and Fair workers taking their breaks. Finally the woman stopped at a door in the back of a small, squat structure and motioned to the children to go inside.

Jack figured she was taking them to some kind of guard post where they'd be questioned. The fellow from the ticket booth at the Temple of Mirth would likely be there, too, and tell the guards what they'd done. Then it would be all over. They'd be ejected from the Fair. Or even taken to the police, who would give them over to Miss DeHaven. . . .

But then the woman pulled aside a curtain, and there were no guards—the room wasn't an office at all. It was some kind of parlor, with Oriental rugs scattered all over the floor. Elaborately patterned tapestries and drapes hung on all sides so that it seemed like they were inside an exotic tent instead of a room. *What is this place?* Jack wondered.

"I'm sorry!" Harold cried suddenly. "It's all
my fault! I ran inside the funhouse without paying
because I was scared of the clown! And then we
were in the maze of mirrors and we wanted to get
out!"

"We'll go back to the Temple of Mirth and pay
what we owe," Alexander offered.

The woman shook her head. "They are fools. You
owe them nothing."

"W-what do you mean?" Frances stammered.

"I mean it is no wonder you want to leave the
Temple of Mirth!" the woman declared. "No wonder the little boy is frightened of the great big ugly
clown face!"

Jack could hear just the faintest trace of an accent
in the woman's speech. It wasn't German or Russian
or Irish. It sounded a little like the accent of a man
who had a pushcart on Jack's street back in New
York. The man sold sweet cakes and bottles of rose
water, but Jack couldn't remember where he'd come
from.

The woman went on. "Who in their right mind
wishes to walk in the labyrinth of mirrors? So many
mirrors facing each other, such bad luck! No wonder

you would wish to leave such a place! Is not a place of *mirth*. Bah!"

"Were . . . were you *helping* us just now?" Jack asked.

"Yes!" cried the woman. "Of course I help you. Every day I walk past that infernal place and see the people come out. They are green in the face. The little children, they are crying from fright. They all waste their ten cents. The man who runs that place, Mr. Fernand, he is a scoundrel!"

At the mention of the name *Mr. Fernand*, Jack saw Frances's eyebrows go up, and Jack knew what he had to ask. "So . . . there's no Mr. McGee there?"

The woman looked at Jack with a curious expression. "There's no Mr. McGee, my child. Not anymore. But you may call me Madame Zee."

Jack's head started to spin. *No Mr. McGee?* Maybe she thought he was talking about someone else. At any rate, they had reached a dead end here. "Um . . . well, thank you for all your help, Madame Zee. . . ."

"We really appreciate it," Alexander added. "But we ought to go. We need to—"

"Oh! Do not leave!" Madame Zee said suddenly. "You must stay." She lowered her voice. "I see how your clothes are. I think you have had some hard times and that you are on your own, yes?"

Eli nodded. But Frances seemed more suspicious. "Why would you help us?" she asked.

Madame Zee sighed and sat down on the parlor couch. "So many people come to me for help. I tell them their fortunes. They always want to find something that they've lost, or someone who is gone." She looked down at her hands and her voice grew softer. "All I can give them are words. I tell them things that will happen in their lives."

"You mean, you give them warnings?" Jack asked.

Madame Zee shook her head no. "I do not call them warnings. People don't like those. You give them a warning, they think it will not happen to them. My own son, for instance. He went to work for some bad people. I tell him he will get hurt! But he never listened. . . ." She took a deep breath. "Never mind. I will not speak of sad things now. Anyway. I do not warn people anymore. I simply tell them things I think will happen."

"And do they really?" Harold asked.

Madame Zee shrugged. "I never know. The people come for their fortunes and then they leave. But you children, I can give you a place to sleep, offer you food, mend your clothes. These are *real* things! And then . . ." She looked right at Jack again. "You remind me of someone I used to know."

Jack felt self-conscious under her steady gaze. "I do?"

"Yes," she said, her voice quavering and her eyes starting to fill with tears. "Someone I miss very much."

Jack didn't know what to do. He noticed Frances had narrowed her eyes the way she did when she didn't quite trust something, and Alexander and Eli wore skeptical looks. Jack had heard about fortune-tellers—they were supposed to be charlatans who couldn't really predict the future. Madame Zee had practically admitted that herself when she said she didn't know if the things she foretold ever really happened! So it was very possible that those tears of hers were just an act. *Right?*

He was still considering this when Harold broke away from Frances's side and ran over to the sofa. "My name is Harold and I'm sorry you are sad." He opened his arms and gave her a big hug. Clearly *he* believed Madame Zee.

Madame Zee wiped her tears and smiled. "Thank you, young Harold. Now, the rest of you, what are *your* names? And you will stay here, yes?"

Jack exchanged looks with Alexander, who shrugged. Frances rolled her eyes, and Eli gave a crooked half smile that seemed to say, *Guess we're stuck here.* The older boys hadn't given a signal yet, after all, and the reward was still waiting. And they couldn't very well leave Harold behind.

"Yes," Jack told her. "We'll stay."

20
THE PORCELAIN HAND

Madame Zee brought out a pitcher of cold water and some paper cups, and then a washbasin and cloth so that they could freshen up. Frances scrubbed her own face and then Harold's.

"Frannie, don't be mad," Harold whispered. "Madame Zee seems really nice."

"Let's just be careful," Frances warned. "She's still a stranger."

While the others took their turns washing up, Frances looked around. The parlor they were in appeared to be a back room. A set of tied-back drapes marked the entry into another room—which, judging by all the odd bric-a-brac on a table in there, was likely where the fortune-telling took place—and beyond that was the open front entrance. There was a velvet rope hanging across to prevent fairgoers from coming in, but Frances could see people strolling past in the late afternoon sunlight and faintly hear the hubbub of the Pike beyond all the draperies.

"Just a moment," Madame Zee said as she went behind a partitioned screen. "I must get ready for work."

Frances still didn't trust Madame Zee, kind as she seemed, so she supposed this was a good moment to take a closer look at some of the stuff in the front room. She motioned for the others to join. "Look at all this hocus-pocus stuff!" she whispered to Jack. On the table was a stack of cards with strange pictures on them and a crystal ball on an iron stand. A tiny plaque on the stand read MADAME ZOGBHI. Frances had no idea how a name like that was pronounced. No wonder this woman had everyone call her Madame Zee—the *zee* was really just the first initial of her last name, and it was probably easier.

"Hey! I found something!" Jack had picked up something from the top of a cabinet next to the table. It was a model of a hand—life-size—cast in white porcelain. It stood straight up on a base just below its wrist, looking as if it could wave hello.

But that wasn't the most curious thing about it.

The lines of the palm were marked in black paint, with labels such as LINE OF FORTUNE, LINE OF HEART, and LINE OF HEAD. The fingers were marked MER-CURY, APOLLO, SATURN, JUPITER. And then symbols were scattered across the whole hand.

"I guess it's a guide for reading palms," Frances said.

"I know, but look at the symbols!" Jack turned the hand over and over. "These are on the medal-lion! And remember I told you I saw some of the symbols carved into a trunk on the boat? They're on this thing, too!"

Alexander came over and looked at the hand too. "We should ask Madame Zee."

"Ask me what?" Madame Zee said as she came out from the back room. She had wrapped a silk scarf around her forehead, and her dark hair hung loose. Over her shirtwaist she'd donned a robe embroi-dered with stars, and she wore a necklace made from thin gold coins. She looked more like a fortune-teller now, though Frances figured it was all still an act if she needed a costume.

Madame Zee saw Jack holding the porcelain hand. "Oh! You wish to know about palmistry, yes? Many secrets are revealed in the hand." She took the porcelain hand from Jack and began to point out some of the features. "These are the lines, and these are the mounts. . . ."

"What about the symbols?" Frances asked.

"Ah, yes. They are for the constellations in the sky. We are born under certain stars. Some people, they are born under the stars of Taurus the Bull—"

Madame Zee paused, for a short bald man had approached the velvet rope at the entrance. "Hey, Catherine!" he called. "I don't suppose you could lend us a hand over at Streets of Cairo?"

Madame Zee gave him a smirk. "*Again?* And close my place for the night?"

"Aw, you know how it is," the short bald man said. "Maloof didn't show up again, and they need someone to talk to the musicians. You know the language. We'll give you Maloof's wages and some of the tips, too."

"All right," Madame Zee replied. "Is such good money, I cannot say no. I will be there soon." The man walked off and she turned to the children. "These fools, they pay me too well. I must go for a while."

"But will you tell us more about these symbols?" Jack asked.

Madame nodded. "I will tell you everything. Maybe I will train you so you can run this place while I go help these dunces over at the Streets of Cairo! But for now, you stay and rest. I will return." She unhooked the velvet rope and stepped outside.

"One more thing!" Frances called. "Your first name is *Catherine*?"

"My second husband, he was American," Madame Zee said with a shrug. "So I took American name when I marry him. Pretty name, you think?"

"Yes," Frances replied, and Jack nodded, too. They had so many more questions, but Madame Zee was hurrying off down the Pike, where the electric lights at the entrances to all the attractions were starting to glow brighter as the daylight faded.

The children returned to the back room and settled into a corner that was strewn with rugs and cushions surrounding a low table. There was a small electric lamp overhead, and everything felt soft and cozy. Frances felt Harold slouching against her the way he did when he was tired, and Jack and Alexander appeared to be sleepy, too. But Eli still looked alert—he actually looked nervous.

Jack noticed, too. "Are you all right, Eli?"

Frances knew that Eli was a little superstitious

about the medallion, and she wondered if he was uncomfortable being here in the fortune-teller's parlor.

Eli took a deep breath. "I found something I forgot about. I've had it in my pocket this whole time, and it slipped my mind that I even put it there! It could have gotten us into big trouble if someone discovered I had it."

"What is it?" Frances asked, but Eli was already reaching into his jacket pocket. He pulled out a small bottle and set it on the table. The label said PURE GIN.

"The gin!" Jack exclaimed. "From the steamboat! From when we were hiding down by the crates!"

"I took this bottle out of the crate to see what it was," Eli explained. "Then the deckhands came by and almost found us. I guess I was so shook up that I just put it in my pocket. And then I forgot all about it."

Frances picked up the bottle. The label had some tiny print with lots of misspelled words. IMPORTD FROM EROUPE. PREMIUN SPIRITS. She didn't drink gin, of course, but even if she did she had a feeling she wouldn't trust *this* stuff. "We'd better throw it out the first chance we get."

"Good thing nobody else discovered you had it,"

Jack told Eli. "Can you imagine if the guards had caught us at the Temple of Mirth, instead of Madame Zee? They would have searched us."

"We're all really lucky," Alexander pointed out. "And speaking of Madame Zee, do you suppose she's originally from Egypt?"

"She must be, if she's helping out at the Streets of Cairo exhibit," Frances said.

"Guess that's why they call it the 'World's Fair,'" Eli said. "There's folks from all over the world here, and they're trying to make everything look like a different country."

Eli was right, Frances realized. The fake mountain was meant to look like Germany, and out on the Pike they'd seen signs for places called IRISH VILLAGE, MYSTERIOUS ASIA, SIBERIAN RAILWAY.

"I know it's supposed to feel like we're traveling the world," said Frances. "But really, it sort of feels like we're in a big circus."

"Or even a zoo," Jack added. "Did you hear about that tribe they brought here from the Philippines? There was someone in line at the peanut cart talking about them. How everyone just goes and gawks."

"Well, I want to say hello to them," Harold murmured, still leaning against Frances. "Maybe they are nice." He sat up straight now. "I think the World's Fair is like a really big Wanderville."

Alexander grinned. "It sort of is, isn't it? It's like a town made of dreams."

Frances nodded. "And all these places where you can go and pretend you're somewhere else . . ."

"Or where you can make it feel like home," Harold said, sleepily. He glanced up at Frances. "Can we go over by the palaces tomorrow . . . and find Wanderville there?" he asked, his words getting slower.

Frances eyed the faces of the others. Jack, Alexander, and Eli all looked as exhausted as she felt, and uncertain, too. There'd been no signal yet from Dutch and his friends, and they still hadn't found the Temple of Promises or Moses McGee. But she had a feeling that they were getting closer.

"I don't know," she told him. "But I do know that the next chance we get, we'll build a palace in Wanderville."

"Okay," Harold mumbled.

After a moment, Frances could hear him snoring softly. Across from her, the boys were stretching out on the rugs and pillows.

Good idea, she thought as she curled up next to her brother. Then she was asleep, too.

Frances dreamed they'd discovered the Temple of Promises, which was like the beautiful domed palace she'd seen when they'd first arrived at the Fair. But when she went inside it was full of mud, and her feet were stuck, and across the room Mr. Zogby and his car were stuck, too, with Dutch and Finn and Chicks and Owney trying to help him. Then suddenly the car's motor was going but making an awful sound: *Bap! BAP! BAP! BAP! BAP!*

Frances shook herself awake. But the noise continued. *BAP! BAP! BAP! BAP!*

When it stopped, Frances sighed and rubbed her eyes. But after a few moments it started again, only not quite as loudly, as if it were not quite as close.

She figured it out. *Someone is hammering something.* Someone was going up and down the Pike with a hammer and nails!

She looked around. Madame Zee wasn't there, but nearby the boys were stirring awake—they must have heard the hammering, too.

"What's that noise?" Alexander muttered.

Frances stood up. "I'll go check." She went through the curtain to the front room. The entrance had been closed for the night with a large sliding door. Frances pushed it aside enough to peer out. It was morning, and she supposed the Fair had recently opened for the day. She heard the hammering noise again and spotted a workman going from building to building, nailing up a poster or notice of some kind. She took a step outside and saw that one had been nailed to the door.

The first four rows of type were the boldest, with letters like a wall of bricks, and reading them felt like she'd hit that wall, straight on.

REWARD
9 YOUTHS AT LARGE!
INCORRIGIBLE—WILD—DEFIANT
HAVE YOU SEEN THEM?

Frances's hands shook as she ripped the poster down.

21
INCORRIGIBLE, WILD, AND DEFIANT

"**H**ow do you know it's about us?" Jack asked.

"Read the whole thing," Frances insisted, shoving the poster at him. "Then read it aloud."

Jack laid it out on the parlor table and pored over the fresh print:

REWARD
9 YOUTHS AT LARGE!
INCORRIGIBLE—WILD—DEFIANT
HAVE YOU SEEN THEM?

SPECIAL EXPOSITION NOTICE

Mr. Edwin Adolphius and the Society for Children's Aid and Relief are offering a generous reward for the apprehension of several waifs who

*have taken leave of their guardians and are
believed to be on the grounds of the Fair.*

*They are responsible for many acts of
property damage and hooliganism aboard the
steamboat* Addie Dauphin*! They are:*

4 boys, ages 14 to 15, very rough in nature

*3 boys, aged about 12, two hailing from the
gangs of New York, one a sharecropper runaway*

*1 girl, age 11, wearing breeches, very
hoydenish in appearance*

*1 boy, age 7, bright auburn hair, possibly a
hostage*

*Report all sightings to Mr. E. Adolphius, c/o
the Southern Hotel.*

Jack felt sick to his stomach. He had had a feeling Edwin Adolphius would come after them, but he had no idea it would be like *this*.

"They called me *hoydenish*!" Frances shook her head in disbelief.

"Only because you wear breeches," Alexander said. "But you're not a hoyden! You're . . . uh, very refined and proper. Even when you don't wear a dress."

The look on Frances's face changed from angry to slightly suspicious. "Well, I couldn't care less what anyone says about *me*," she said quickly, looking down at the poster again. "But why does this poster call Harold a possible hostage?"

"So that people will think we're dangerous," Jack said indignantly. "It's all just a ploy!"

Eli grinned. "So you and Alexander aren't really from New York gangs?"

"I bet Dutch and his friends would be impressed," Frances said with a snort.

"But wait!" said Jack, suddenly reminded. "Do you suppose they're all right? They're mentioned on this poster, too. What if they've been caught already?"

Alexander rubbed his head. "If they're still hiding out by the gates, they might be safe."

"But then again, they might not even know that there's a search out for all of us," Frances pointed out. "We need to go warn them!"

"Good idea." Jack glanced around the parlor. "We should also talk to Madame Zee! But where is she?" He was still hoping she'd tell them more about the mysterious symbols. Maybe he could even show her the medallion.

"Do you suppose she came back here during the night?" Frances went over to where they had been sleeping. Harold had been the last to awaken, and he was sitting up now with a small fringed blanket draped over his shoulders. "Look." Frances picked up the blanket. "This wasn't here when we went to sleep. She must have covered Harold up. Maybe she's out getting breakfast."

"What if she sees the poster?" Jack fretted. "We need to find a way to explain it to her."

"It might be too late," Eli said. He pointed to the low table next to Harold. "Remember we left the gin bottle there? It's gone now!"

Frances's eyes got wide. "Madame Zee took the gin?"

They looked all around the parlor and checked the front room. But the bottle couldn't be found.

"Maybe she just likes gin," Harold said.

"Or maybe we're already in trouble," Jack said. His head was reeling as he imagined Madame Zee marching to the nearest guards' station. They'd meant to throw out that bottle, but the fact that they had it in their possession made them sound just like the "incorrigible" kids that poster claimed they were. And now Madame Zee had the bottle as evidence.

"I should have never picked up that stupid thing in the first place!" Eli moaned. "We'd better leave. Madame Zee could be turning us in right now!"

"And we ought to find Dutch and Finn and the others and warn them about the poster," Jack added. He hoped it wasn't too late for them.

They started for the back door, but Frances said, "Wait!" and dashed behind the partitioned screen that Madame Zee had changed behind the night before.

"What are you doing?" Jack said, eyeing the door anxiously. "We have to get out of here!"

"But we also have to make sure nobody spots us!" Frances called back. "Everyone will be on the lookout for a girl in breeches!"

A moment later Frances emerged, wearing what appeared to be a gypsy's dress with a spangled sash.

Jack had to bite his lip to keep from laughing. "You look crazy."

"It's the only thing that was short enough in the skirt." Frances sighed.

"No, you're perfect!" Alexander said. He turned red for some reason. "I mean . . . there are all these costumed dancers here at the Fair and . . . and you look just like one of them. You'll blend right in."

Just then Jack remembered something else. "What about Harold?" he asked. "The poster mentioned his red hair. How do we hide *that*?"

They all studied Harold as he wiped his nose on his sleeve. Somehow, Jack thought, his hair seemed brighter than ever. "Do we have to walk by the clown head again?" Harold asked.

"You know what, Harold?" Frances said. "Maybe it's better if you just stay here and hide for now."

With all the hanging draperies, it wasn't hard to find a corner in the front room where Harold could sit unseen, close enough to the front entrance to make an escape if necessary.

"Sit tight until we come get you," Frances explained. "I'll call you from outside and you can slip out." Harold nodded, and Frances hugged him tightly.

At last Jack slid open the door at the front entrance. "Let's go!" he whispered. He hoped they could get to Dutch, Finn, Chicks, and Owney in time.

It didn't seem safe for the four of them to walk down the Pike together, since people seeking the reward from the poster would likely be looking for a group of children.

Jack eyed the crowded avenue. "Two of us should walk ahead."

"You and Eli go first," Alexander said. "Frances and I can follow a little ways behind you."

"You do that, Alex," Eli said with just the slightest smirk on his face.

Jack wanted to ask Eli what he thought was so funny, but as they joined the throngs of fairgoers walking along the Pike, his attention shifted as he realized they'd lost their bearings. Yesterday Madame Zee had led them to the fortune-teller's building from a back alley, but now they were in the middle of the Pike, which appeared to stretch half a mile in either direction.

Jack looked behind him. Frances and Alexander had the guidebook with the map, which they were anxiously studying. They seemed lost, too. The fake mountain where the older boys were hiding was at one end of the Pike—but which end?

"I see it!" Eli said, pointing to the east. "The mountain! Let's go!"

They strode as fast as they could go without running. The Pike seemed to be getting busier by the

minute, with barkers in front of every other amuse-
ment, and after every few steps music or cheers
would burst from some entrance or gathered crowd
nearby. But Jack tried to keep his gaze straight ahead.
He didn't want to risk making eye contact with anyone, lest someone guess that he and Eli were two of
the children "at large."

Eli stopped abruptly. "Hey!" he said.

Jack froze, ready to run if he had to. "What is it?"

"Remember how I heard that some of my mama's
kin were working here at the Fair?"

Jack nodded.

"Well, that's my cousin Willie over there, I know
it!" Eli pointed across the avenue to a teenage boy
who was setting up chairs at an outdoor restaurant.

Before Jack could reply, Frances and Alexander
caught up with him and Eli. They were half out of
breath.

"The signal!" Frances said, panting.

"The flag!" Alexander added. "It's up! On the
mountain!"

Jack looked up at the top of the fake mountain.
He hadn't been able to make it out before, but now
that they were closer he could see, sure enough, a

stick jutting out of one of the highest crags. A stick with a bandana tied to it like a flag.

"Uh-oh," Jack whispered.

"Do you think the boys are still hiding?" Eli wondered. "I don't see them up there."

"And do you suppose the signal means they saw Miss DeHaven coming through the front gate?" Frances asked. "Or Edwin Adolphius? Or both?"

"*Edwin Adolphius,*" Alexander said, his face pale as he looked past Jack.

"What?" Jack asked.

"Don't turn around," Alexander whispered. "Just run."

22
THE NAME ON THE CURTAIN

Frances was glad she hadn't picked a longer dress from among Madame Zee's things. If she had, she might not have been able to run so fast! But even still, the Pike was getting so busy that they could only move in short bursts, dashing from one clearing in the crowd to another.

The four of them darted into a side passage next to an exhibit called Fair Japan.

"Did he . . . see us?" Jack asked as he tried to catch his breath.

Frances nodded. Her stomach had had a twisted-up feeling from the moment she and Alexander had spotted Edwin Adolphius. His eyes had met theirs, and she'd seen the spark of recognition through his beady stare.

"So what do we do now?" Eli asked.

"It's too late to warn Dutch and the others about the poster," Alexander pointed out. "We have to hide."

"And we have to get Harold!" Frances said. She thought of him hiding back at Madame Zee's. Her brother couldn't sit still for more than half an hour—how long had it been since they'd left? She peered around the corner and looked up and down the Pike.

"Be careful!" Jack whispered. "Adolphius might see you! I don't think we've lost him yet!"

Frances didn't see Edwin Adolphius. But what she *did* see was a crowd forming on the walkway in front of Madame Zee's place. A *big* crowd—around the place where she'd left Harold!

What is happening? Frances felt her heart thudding as she bolted around the corner toward Madame Zee's.

By the time she reached the crowd, Alexander, Jack, and Eli had caught up.

"What's going on?" Alexander asked, but Frances didn't know. The crowd ran the length of the entrance to Madame Zee's and was already four deep. Frances stood on her toes to get a better view and saw that the velvet ropes had been used to make a space between the threshold of Madame Zee's and the crowd. A space, Frances realized, like a stage. A set of painted curtains concealed the entrance.

Frances chewed her lip nervously. Her brother didn't seem to be anywhere in the crowd, so she crossed her fingers and hoped that he was still hiding inside. She'd sneak in there soon enough, as soon as this *thing*—whatever it was—was over.

"Excuse me," Frances said to a woman who stood next to her adjusting her straw hat. "Is this some kind of show?"

"It's a demonstration," the woman whispered. "On the mysteries of the ancient realm."

"Oh." Frances had no idea what that meant.

"No, I heard it's a séance," a man nearby said. "And somebody gets hypnotized."

"Oh, that's over at the Moorish Palace, and that's all fake," the straw-hatted woman replied. "*This* lady is for real. They say you won't be able to believe your own eyes!"

Frances tried to get as close to the velvet rope as she could. She looked around and saw that the boys had done the same thing in different spots across the crowd. Jack was gesturing frantically, trying to get her attention.

What? Frances mouthed.

Look! Jack mouthed back, motioning to the curtain.

Frances craned her neck to make out the words on the curtain. *The Mesmeric Marvels of Madame Zogbhi,* they read. She still didn't know how to pronounce that name, but something about it made her brain itch. She just shrugged back at Jack, who looked frustrated.

"What is this place, anyway?" Frances asked the straw-hatted woman.

"Why, it's the Temple of Palmistry," the woman replied.

Frances blinked. Suddenly her brain was getting even itchier.

"Excuse me, could you say that again?" Frances asked the woman.

The woman sighed. "The Temple of Palmistry. Do you have a Fair guide? There's an ad for it in there."

The guide! Frances's heart raced as she tried to remember who had the little booklet. *Alexander's got it!* She made her way as quickly as she could to his spot in the crowd, only a few feet away from the velvet rope. "Sorry," she whispered as she nudged and stumbled. The crowd was becoming denser, and she had a feeling the show would start any minute. But she had to see for herself . . .

"What are you doing?" Alexander asked as Frances practically yanked the guide out of his pocket and started flipping through the pages.

"I think we've found the Temple of Promises!" Frances said. "Look! It wasn't shown on the map, but it's advertised here!"

She pointed to the page:

THE TEMPLE OF PALMISTRY

MRS. CATHERINE MCGEE, PROPRIETOR.
DIVINATIONS, FORTUNES, AND EXHIBITIONS OF
ANCIENT MYSTERIES
SO REMARKABLE AS TO CONVINCE THE MOST
SKEPTICAL.
LOCATED ON THE PIKE

"Do you see?" Frances asked him. "It's not the Temple of *Promises*, but—"

"The Temple of *Palmistry*!" Alexander finished. "And it wasn't *Moses* McGee we were looking for, but *Mrs. McGee!*"

Frances nodded. "We'd just heard the words wrong! And Mrs. McGee is Madame Zee, isn't it?"

she said, suddenly making the connection. "She said her name was Catherine!"

"There she is now!" Alexander whispered. Frances looked up in just time to see Madame Zee step out from between the curtains, wearing a robe that was even more resplendent than the one she'd donned the night before.

"Good day, ladies and gentlemen," she said. "Welcome to the Temple of Palmistry, and I am . . ." She pointed to the words painted on the curtain. "Madame Zogbhi."

Frances's jaw dropped when she heard the name spoken. It was pronounced *Zogby*!

She turned to Alexander, who looked just as confused as she felt. "But how . . ." he mumbled. Frances knew what he was wondering: *What was the connection?*

She searched for Jack in the crowd, because she suddenly understood why he had been waving and pointing at the curtain—*he'd* figured out the significance of "Zogbhi" first! She wondered what else Jack had figured out.

But when she spotted him again, he wasn't alone. Edwin Adolphius held him firmly by the forearm.

"Oh, no!" Frances could barely breathe out the

words. "Jack's caught!" She and Alexander watched helplessly as Jack struggled and tried to yank his arm free. "What should we do?"

"Shh!" scolded a man standing behind Frances. "The show is starting!"

Madame Zee was speaking. "Today, I will demonstrate to you the remarkable powers of the constellations and the marvels that manifest themselves when the mind is harnessed to the infinite wisdom of the ancient stars." She went over to the curtain. "Behold!"

Frances kept her eyes on Jack and Edwin Adolphius, even as she could hear the curtains part.

A gasp rose up from the crowd, and Mr. Adolphius turned his head to look at the action on the stage.

At that moment, Jack wrenched his arm free and darted under the velvet rope. But even *he* stopped and stared at what the curtains had just revealed.

What is going on?

Frances finally turned and saw for herself.

Just inside the entrance to Madame Zee's, Harold sat on a wooden chair. It looked like an ordinary chair, except that it was tilted back and balanced on a single chair leg.

Or rather, a single chair leg that just happened to be balanced on a wooden ball that gently rocked back and forth.

"Impossible!" someone in the crowd exclaimed.

Yet Harold sat on top of it all, defying gravity, grinning widely.

23
THE AMULET OF THE EASTERN SKY

"Hi, Jack!" Harold called when he saw Jack standing by the curtains.

Jack's mouth was too dry to answer. His arm smarted from where Edwin Adolphius had gripped it while hissing, *You're coming with me.* Now Jack's instincts were screaming, *Run, hide,* but everything around him was oddly still, almost frozen. A few in the crowd murmured and whispered in amazement at Harold and his teetering chair, but everyone else seemed to be holding their breath. Any disruption, it seemed, would break the illusion.

But then Madame Zee caught Jack's eye.

"Ah, yes," she said, loud enough for the audience to hear. "And now my four young assistants shall come forward. Please, you will let them through."

One by one, Alexander, Eli, and Frances emerged from the crowd and slipped under the velvet rope to the stage area. Jack was grateful for Madame Zee's quick thinking in calling them "assistants." Frances even looked the part in her borrowed gypsy dress.

Madame Zee directed them to stand off to the side near Jack. "My dear assistants," she said. "You know this little boy, do you not?" She motioned to Harold, who waved.

The audience remained rapt. Jack could see Edwin Adolphius glowering at him and his friends. But being on stage in plain sight seemed the safest place to be at the moment. As long as the show went on, that is.

"Yes, ma'am," Jack answered Madame Zee as the others nodded. "We know him."

"And does he possess any special powers that you are aware of?" Madame asked.

Frances appeared to be holding back a grin, but she answered, "No, ma'am."

Madame Zee smiled. "So then he is an ordinary child," she announced to the crowd. "No different than the children right here."

"*Trouble* is what they are!" Mr. Adolphius's voice rumbled up out of the audience. He shook a fist and pointed indignantly to the stage while the onlookers around him turned to glare at the disruption.

"*HUSH!*" scolded a stout woman next to him. More reprimands and shushing came from all around. Mr. Adolphius went silent and pulled his hat lower over his eyes.

"As I was saying," Madame Zee continued. "This boy is ordinary. He is no magician, has no unusual abilities. But it is the radiance of the ancient stars, whose invisible powers I have summoned today, that keep him suspended!"

The front row of the audience leaned in over the velvet rope for a closer look.

"You must not get too close," Madame Zee warned. "The field of radiance is very strong. It does not touch the boy, but surrounds him."

As Jack watched, he suspected there was another reason why Madame Zee didn't want the crowd to get closer. From where he stood, he could just barely make out a few faint glints above Harold's chair that he suspected were thin wires. He glanced over at Madame Zee, who winked at him.

"It is the mystics of Egypt who taught me to channel these ancient powers," she told the audience.

Then she reached into her robe and pulled out a hidden necklace from around her neck.

It was the medallion! Jack nearly stopped breathing. Or rather, he realized quickly, Madame Zee's amulet looked just like the medallion in his pocket.

"This is the Amulet of the Eastern Sky," Madame Zee announced. "I am using it to direct the radiance." She turned and held out her amulet in the direction of Harold and his chair. "Much as a lens directs a beam of light."

The crowd began to murmur as, slowly but smoothly, Harold's chair lifted into the air. The one leg it balanced on suddenly floated free, and the wooden ball rolled away. Harold's eyes popped wider in surprise as the chair gently straightened itself.

A burst of applause went up from the crowd and Jack could hear words of amazement all around him. "Incredible!" "How does she do it?" "Unbelievable!"

"Is it true," called out a man behind Jack, "that you can make that chair fly through the air?"

"I heard she did it at the World's Fair in Chicago!" someone else called out. "There was a different boy, of course."

Madame Zee turned to face the audience and let

the amulet drop back against her chest. "It is true," she said. "Eleven years ago, I gave this very demonstration with another boy. My son. He knew something of these ancient arts that I practice, and he had in his possession another amulet, the Amulet of the Western Sky. With both amulets, the power of the radiance was twofold!"

She straightened up and took a deep breath. "Now there is only the one amulet. The other one . . ." Her voice faltered just slightly, but it was enough to make Jack's heart pound. "It was with my son. But he and his amulet are gone."

Was, Madame Zee had said. As if her son were no longer alive. Jack could see it in her face. He knew her look: It was the same one his mother had worn in the weeks after Daniel was gone.

It was grief.

Madame Zee touched the amulet around her neck. "These amulets, they have the power to guide us. But they are not strong enough," she said, "to protect us."

Jack's throat felt tight, even though there were so many things he needed to say. Because now he knew who Madame Zee really was.

The crowd had fallen silent. Jack glanced up and

saw Frances looking at him, her eyes imploring him to *speak up*! She must have figured it out, too. Jack began to search his pockets. . . .

The voice that broke the silence came from behind them. "Madame Zee?"

It was Harold. "Madame Zee," he said again. "Don't be sad. Um, I think it protected him. The amulet, that is."

Madame Zee turned to stare at Harold. "My child, what do you mean?"

The medallion—the *amulet*—was in Jack's hand. He held it out and stepped toward Madame Zee.

"Is this the Amulet of the Western Sky?" he asked her.

She reached out with a shaking hand, and Jack pressed it into her palm.

For a moment her only response was to nod. She wiped her tearing eyes on the back of her hand. "But how did . . . ?"

"Philander Zogby gave us this two days ago," Jack told her.

"*My son!*" Madame Zee cried. "He's alive?"

At that same moment Harold's chair dropped to the floor with a thud. The audience gasped.

But Harold, unhurt, climbed off the chair. He ran and gave Madame Zee a big hug as the crowd broke into applause.

"Mr. Zogby is nice," he told Madame Zee. "I'm glad you're his mother."

24

THE SIGN OF THE BULL AND THE SIGN OF THE SCORPION

"Mrs. Zogbhi," Frances began, as the crowd began to disperse. "I mean, Madame Zogbhi—"

"I insist you still call me Madame Zee. Everyone who knows me does," the woman said. "Only strangers call me Mrs. McGee." She motioned behind her to the entrance of the Temple of Palmistry. "And they think I must have a husband who runs this place, so they are always asking for *Mr.* McGee too."

She winked at Frances, who turned red as she remembered that *they* had originally been looking for a Mr. McGee as well.

"But never mind that," Madame Zee told her. "You must tell me everything about my son!"

"First we saw Mr. Zogby in a motorcar!" Harold began. "And the car was stuck in the mud—"

"Harold, not now," Frances broke in. She looked at Madame Zee. "We have plenty to tell you, but right now there's someone looking for us."

"I see that," Madame Zee said as Edwin Adolphius stepped over the velvet rope and strode toward them.

"There they are!" Mr. Adolphius cried. Behind him was a young man with a curled mustache whose badge read JEFFERSON GUARD—OFFICIAL SECURITY—LOUISIANA PURCHASE EXPOSITION.

Frances instinctively reached for Harold, while Jack and the other boys turned in every direction, searching for a possible escape. But she could see it was useless to run now.

"Very well, Mr. Adolphius," the guard replied. "I'll whistle for more guards to help round them up."

"That won't be necessary," Madame Zee said. "I've already sent for the police."

What? Frances couldn't believe it, and she could see the shock on Jack's face, too. What was Madame Zee doing?

The fortune-teller had stepped closer to Mr. Adolphius, and she gave him a cool smile. "You are Edwin Adolphius, the great industrialist, yes?" she asked. "You have many factories. You command many steamboats."

Mr. Adolphius smiled and stroked his beard, clearly flattered. "Why, yes. Well, I don't *command* the steamboats, but I do *own* them."

"And you are in a charge of all that happens on them?"

"Of course!" he said proudly.

Just then two uniformed men approached their group. Frances swallowed hard at the sight of them— St. Louis police officers!

"Thank you for coming, Sergeant," Madame Zee said to the older one as both officers tipped their caps politely.

"Ordinarily I don't have jurisdiction here at the World's Fair, but this is a special case. You said you had something important to show us, Mrs. McGee?" the sergeant asked.

"Indeed," Madame Zee said, as she pulled out an object from her robe.

Frances recognized it right away. *The gin bottle!*

"That's stolen property!" Mr. Adolphius said. "These children stole it from the *Addie Dauphin*!"

"Is that so?" the police sergeant said. "Well, we

checked the cargo manifest on your steamboat when it came in today, and we sure didn't see any shipments of gin listed."

"I don't see what any of that has to do with the matter at hand!" Mr. Adolphius raged. "These children are thieves, and that bottle is proof!"

The younger officer shrugged. "That's not why Mrs. McGee called us today. Seems she'd seen a bottle like this before."

Frances looked over at Jack, who raised an eyebrow in surprise. Madame Zee didn't take the gin bottle to use against *them*—she was using it against Mr. Adolphius!

Madame Zee turned to face Edwin Adolphius. "My son, he worked on your steamboats. Before he went missing, he was working on the *Rochelle*."

Mr. Adolphius waggled a finger. "There now, I'll have you know I *sold* that steamboat a full month before—"

"Before it caught fire and sank?" the sergeant broke in. "Those were very mysterious circumstances, Mr. Adolphius. The *Rochelle* was being used to smuggle untaxed liquor and fruit all up and down the Mississippi."

"And we have reason to believe the same thing has

been happening on the *Addie Dauphin*," the younger officer added. "Isn't that right, Mrs. McGee?"

Madame Zee nodded and motioned toward Harold. "That's what this little boy told me," she said.

"I told her how the gin was hidden inside the cotton on the boat," Harold said. "And those barrels of rum, too. And they didn't want us to see them!"

"This is outrageous!" Mr. Adolphius fumed. "You have no proof!"

"You said that last time, when we were questioning you about the sinking of the *Rochelle*," the sergeant said. "But this time"—he held up the gin bottle—"we've got evidence. And witnesses. We've got officers talking to other passengers on the *Addie Dauphin* right now."

Alexander leaned over to Frances. "Are you following this conversation?" he whispered.

Frances nodded. "I think Edwin Adolphius is a smuggler. And the police have been trying to catch him in the act. . . ."

Jack leaned in. "And now they've got him!"

"Yes," Frances murmured in amazement. "They've got him all right."

Edwin Adolphius's face had turned deep red with rage as the younger police officer locked brass handcuffs onto his wrists. With his black and white beard, his face seemed to become a garish mask that Frances would have found terrifying if she hadn't been so relieved.

"Send for my lawyers!" Mr. Adolphius told the curly-mustached Jefferson Guard. "And my motorcar!"

"And take all those reward posters down," the police sergeant said to the guard, adding, "Adolphius, maybe you were able to pay the fools at the Fair to do your bidding, but you'll get nowhere with me."

Then Edwin Adolphius was led away down the Pike in handcuffs, the two police officers at his sides. The five children and Madame Zee watched them walk all the way past the amusements—the Water Chutes, the Pop Corn Palace, the Battle Abbey— until they disappeared around a corner.

Frances knew there were amazing things to see at the World's Fair, but as far as she was concerned, that was the best sight of all.

Jack turned to Madame Zee.

"You said I reminded you of someone you knew long ago," he said. "Was that someone your son?"

Jack thought he had figured it out. Mr. Zogby had reminded him a lot of his brother, Daniel, so maybe Madame Zee had seen a resemblance in Jack, too.

Madame Zee nodded. "Yes, my boy. All five of you children remind me of Philander in different ways, but you and he have the same look," she said. "You are restless, I think. My son is, too. That is why he got caught up with the bad men." She shook her head. "I warned him to stay away from them, but he liked the money."

The others were also listening to Madame Zee.

"Why did you think he was dead?" Alexander asked her.

She sighed. "My Philander, he told a policeman about the smuggling on Adolphius's steamboats. But he was still working on the boats, too. Of course this was very dangerous. What if Mr. Adolphius discovered my son was betraying him? That would be very bad.

"And then one night, there was a fire on the *Rochelle*. My son, he was on board."

Madame Zee put her hand to her chest, as if she were hearing the news for the first time. "I hear rumors. They say Mr. Adolphius set the fire. But I did not know what happened. All I knew was that Philander didn't come home."

"Maybe he's had to stay away," Frances suggested.

"Right," Eli said. "Maybe he hasn't come home because he doesn't want Mr. Adolphius to find him."

Madame Zee looked down at her hands. "I do not know. I think perhaps he decided to just forget about home. Maybe that is easier for him. At least now I know he is alive."

Jack remembered something just then. "Can I see the Amulet of the Western Sky again? Just for a moment?"

Madame Zee handed it to him.

He found the strange symbol that looked like a loop and showed it to her. "What does this symbol mean?" he asked. "And this one?" He pointed to the symbol that looked like an *M* with an arrow at the end of it. He told her how he had seen them carved into a trunk on the *Addie Dauphin*.

Madame Zee's hand flew up to her face in surprise. "One of those is the sign of the bull. That is the constellation Philander was born under. And the other sign . . ." She took a deep breath and her eyes shone with tears. "That is the sign of the scorpion. It is my sign."

"He was thinking of you," Frances said softly. Next to her, Harold nodded in agreement.

"He didn't want to forget you at all," Jack added. "And he gave us the amulet to give to you, so that you would know he was okay."

"Yes," Madame Zee said. "I think you are right." She wiped her eyes again. "You know, I am a widow two times—the first Mr. Zogby is gone, and then Mr. McGee. But it is hardest of all when you believe your son is lost forever."

It came to Jack suddenly—a memory from New York, in the days after his brother died. How he'd overheard his parents talking not about Daniel, but about him.

I don't want to lose him, too, his mother had said.

And so they had sent him on the orphan train so that he could live.

Jack looked around at Frances and Harold, Eli and Alexander. Then he looked down at the amulet in his hands. So many times in the past few days he had looked at it, hoping it could tell him something.

Now, it seemed, it had.

25
THE REWARD

They were still gathered in front of the Temple of Palmistry when they heard a voice.

"Elijah? Elijah Pike!"

Eli turned. "Willie?" he called back.

Jack turned to see the tall teenage boy Eli had pointed out earlier as his cousin coming up the street toward the temple entrance. He headed straight for Eli, who ran to meet him with a grin.

"I thought that was you walking by the restaurant!" Willie said. "My mama and Aunt Viola have been wondering about you ever since we got word that you left home."

"It's a long story," Eli told him. "But these are my friends." He motioned over to Jack, Frances, Harold, and Alexander. "We've all been traveling together."

"We were on a railroad handcar!" Harold told Willie. "And then in a motorcar. And then a steamboat!"

Willie shook all their hands. "I bet you have some stories," he said to Eli. "I'm done with my shift now. How about I buy you a lemonade and you tell me all about it?"

Eli smiled. "I'll be back in a little bit," he said to Jack. He glanced over at Madame Zee, who was still dabbing her eyes with a handkerchief. "Seems like this day has been all about finding family," he added.

As Jack watched Eli and his cousin make their way to one of the refreshment stands, he realized he still had the amulet in his hand. He took it over to Madame Zee, who was showing the others some of her fortune-telling cards.

"I am glad to have it again," she said. "I tell you truth—these amulets, they are not real gold. They are sold as souvenirs back in Egypt! But it is good for my heart to have this one back."

Harold looked up. "Is it time to give the reward now?" he asked.

Madame Zee's brow furrowed. "Reward?" she asked. "But . . . it is only a trinket. I have no reward to give."

Jack felt his face grow hot. He had forgotten all about the idea of a reward, and now it seemed foolish to ask for one.

"But there is a reward, Harold," Frances said. She crouched down to look eye-to-eye with Harold, and she pulled him close. "Did you see how very glad Madame Zee was when she found out Mr. Zogby was okay?"

Harold nodded quickly. "She was crying. But it was happy crying, and I hugged her."

"That was really nice, wasn't it?"

A smile began to spread over her little brother's face. "Yes."

"Well," Frances said. "I think that was our reward, don't you?"

Harold reached up and gave Madame Zee's hand a squeeze. "Yes!"

Jack could feel himself starting to smile, too. As much as he'd wished for that reward money, maybe Frances was right and what had happened today was enough.

"But, um . . ." Alexander began. He was trying to smile, but it was strained. "The thing is, we promised Dutch and those fellows that we would share the reward with them. And, well, this has been a nice reward, but I don't know how we're going to *share* it. . . ."

"Oh, no," Jack whispered. "Dutch and Finn . . ."

". . . and Owney and Chicks," Harold continued.

"We forgot about them!" Frances cried. "You don't suppose something happened to them after they gave the signal, do you?"

Alexander looked stricken. "We'd better look for them."

"What is wrong?" Madame Zee asked them. "The four of you, you look just like you did when you came out of the Temple of Mirth!"

"We have four friends who might be in trouble," Jack said. "They were hiding out in the Tyrolean Alps. But we don't know if they stayed there!"

Madame Zee was thinking. "I know a good way you get there fast." She pointed down the Pike. "You go behind under and over the sea. There is a back door. Go through, and you'll be in the alley next to the Alps."

The directions made Jack's head spin. *Behind, under, and over the sea?* He couldn't imagine what she possibly meant.

"Go!" Madame said. "Hurry!"

The four children took off running, past the

Ancient Rome exhibit, Hagenbeck's Animals, and Hunting in the Ozarks. The Pike seemed to Jack like an endless river of flickering electric light and calliope music, a river that could swallow them up if they weren't careful.

Suddenly Frances skidded to a stop. "There!" she said, pointing to an arched entrance with the words UNDER & OVER THE SEA on it. Jack nearly laughed out loud. It was another Pike attraction!

"Madame Zee said to go behind it," Jack said. They darted down the side of the building. They passed two women dressed as glittering mermaids, and then a man in a sea-monster costume who nearly dropped his frankfurter sandwich as they ran by.

Finally they were in a dim alleyway that ran between the back of the Pike buildings and the boundary wall of the fairgrounds. Jack could just make out the side of the fake mountain, and they began to walk toward it. But they noticed something else, too, at the end of the alley just below the mountain—something large and dark with touches of glinting brass.

"It's a motorcar!" Harold exclaimed.

It was an impressive car, with a hard top and

glass windows. It was parked just around the bend and was so big they could only see the front half of it—the shining black hood that jutted out into the alley. As the children walked toward it they saw that it was flanked by a man with driving goggles and a uniform—Jack supposed he was the chauffeur—and two Jefferson Guards who stood at attention.

"That car must belong to someone important," Alexander said. "Look at all the guards."

But as they drew closer, Jack realized something. "They're not just guarding the car," he said. "Someone's inside." He could just barely make out four figures through the windows. Then one of them put his hands up to the glass in the side window and peered out at them.

"That's Owney!" Frances whispered.

After a moment they could see Dutch peering out the window too, and then the other two boys. Dutch put his fingers to his lips as if to say, *Be quiet.* Jack could tell the guards hadn't noticed their group coming down the alley yet, but they could at any moment.

"We'd better hide," Jack whispered. He was sure that the car belonged to Edwin Adolphius.

Frances nodded. "Where?"

Jack didn't answer. Because just then another figure emerged from around the corner.

Miss DeHaven walked around the front of the car and faced them. She straightened her beautiful hat and smiled, as if she'd been waiting for them all along.

26
WHAT MISS DEHAVEN DID

"**D**on't *worry*, children," Miss DeHaven said. "We wouldn't *dare* leave without you."

She began to walk toward them slowly and deliberately, then nudged the two guards, who joined her. "In fact, we've been *waiting* for you this whole time," she continued.

With each step of Miss DeHaven's approach, Frances took a step of her own in the opposite direction, pulling Harold along with her. Jack and Alexander did the same thing, each one faced with a guard.

"Just keep backing up," Jack whispered. "Slowly." Frances wanted nothing more than to turn around and run, but maybe Jack had a plan of some kind.

"I *do* hope you had a *delightful* visit here at the

Exposition," Miss DeHaven said. "Your friends here"—she nodded toward the car—"couldn't *resist* leaving their little hiding place to see the sights!"

Frances took another step back, then another, trying to keep Harold shielded behind her. Any moment it seemed Miss DeHaven or the guards might lunge at them, but still they didn't.

She wants *us to run,* Frances realized. Running would cause a scene, attract more of the Jefferson Guards. But as long as they kept moving backward, each step took Miss DeHaven and the guards further from the motorcar where the older boys were being held.

She took another step back as the chaperone moved toward her.

"I *trust* you'll find the industrial school to be *quite* exciting," Miss DeHaven said. "I *do* hope your young brother is willing to work *hard*!"

A cold prickling feeling swept all up and down Frances's arms and she froze in her place. She took a deep breath.

Miss DeHaven stepped forward. And forward again. Harold retreated a few more paces, but Frances stayed where she was.

She stayed rooted there until Miss DeHaven was

right in front of her, looking her up and down the way she had back in New York, the day she'd come to the Howland Mission for Little Wanderers. She'd had no idea who Miss DeHaven was at the time, but Frances often thought about what she would have done if she had known.

Miss DeHaven took one more step.

Frances put her hands out and shoved her as hard as she could.

"Why—YOU!" Miss DeHaven screeched. She staggered backward a few steps on her heels. "You little hellion!"

Frances charged forward and pushed her again. Her eyes burned with hot tears, and the edges of her vision were blurry white. She sensed things happening beyond the white—there were shouts, and the noise of pounding feet—but all she wanted to do was shove and push and shove and shove.

Just then someone grabbed her arm and yanked her away.

"That was really something, Queenie!"

Dutch! The older boys must have seen their chance to escape from the car!

Chicks and Finn and Owney had joined Jack and Alexander in their standoff with the two guards. The two sides glared at each other as if daring the other to make a move. As for Miss DeHaven, she had retreated several paces back and now hung limply on the arm of the chauffeur—though Frances didn't believe for a moment that she was truly feeling faint.

A quick pang of worry hit Frances just then. "Where's Harold?" she gasped. She turned and saw that he'd run back down the alley and was now standing with Eli and his cousin, who she supposed had come looking for them.

Pheee-eeeeee! Someone was blowing a whistle down at the end of the alley.

Another Jefferson Guard had appeared. "*Order!*" he called, and everyone turned.

"Stand down, men," he said to the two guards. "The reward for catching these kids has been cancelled."

The two guards nodded. They shrugged at Jack, Alexander, and the four older boys, who relaxed their stances and breathed sighs of relief.

"What?" Miss DeHaven cried. "What's going on?"

The guard pointed to the motorcar. "Is this Mr. Edwin Adolphius's automobile?"

The chauffeur nodded as the guard approached him and Miss DeHaven.

Frances recognized the guard's curled mustache—he'd been with Mr. Adolphius earlier! He handed a note to the chauffeur, who read it, stunned.

"Give me that!" Miss DeHaven grabbed the note to take a look. After a moment she gasped. "*Arrested? For smuggling?*"

The guard nodded gravely and turned to the chauffeur. "Mr. Adolphius asked that his car be returned to the Southern Hotel."

Miss DeHaven turned the note over, and when she saw the other side was blank she crumpled it and tossed it down. "Did he have any message for *me*?"

The guard and the chauffeur exchanged sheepish looks. "Er . . . no, ma'am."

The color drained from Miss DeHaven's face. But then she seemed to compose herself, reaching up to fix her hat, which had gone askew when Frances had shoved her. "Very well," she muttered.

Frances had been almost holding her breath ever since the guard blew his whistle. But now she met Jack and Alexander's questioning looks—Miss DeHaven couldn't do anything to them now, could she?

"What are *you* filthy brats looking at?" she said, glancing over at Frances and Jack and the others. Miss DeHaven enjoyed being a bully as long as she could threaten to send children to Mr. Adolphius's factory or to the Pratcherd Ranch, but there wasn't much she could do all on her own.

"N-nothing," Alexander said.

Mr. Adolphius's chauffeur dutifully walked over to the back of the car and began to work the crank. Miss DeHaven patted her hat again and looked all around—she seemed nervous, almost fidgety. She opened the small beaded pocketbook she carried, frowned, and then shut it again.

After about a dozen cranks the automobile engine sputtered and then began to chug, with a regular rhythm. Frances watched as the chauffeur detached the crank, then put it away in the trunk.

He looked up as he closed the trunk. "Hey!" he yelled.

Frances turned in time to see Miss DeHaven shut the car door. She'd climbed into the driver's seat.

"She's taking Mr. Adolphius's motorcar!" Jack exclaimed.

Miss DeHaven's face was grimly determined

behind the wheel. The car shot forward, braked abruptly with a screech, then lurched into the alley.

Frances stood frozen in amazement until Alexander grabbed her arm and yanked her over to the edge of the alley with the others, safely out of the way.

"Stop!" the chauffeur bellowed as he lunged into the motorcar's path. But Miss DeHaven steered right around him. Then, with a few more lurches and a sharp *pop*! of the engine, she turned and drove out of the fairground gates.

The three Jefferson Guards grinned and scratched their heads.

"That was the darnedest thing I've ever seen!" said Finn.

"Was that car a Pierce-Arrow?" called Eli's cousin, Willie.

"Report that car stolen!" the chauffeur demanded of the Jefferson Guards.

Frances turned to Alexander and Jack. "Where do you suppose Miss DeHaven's headed?"

"Back to New York?" Alexander guessed.

Frances tried to read Jack's face at the mention of New York, but she couldn't. He gave only a wry smile.

"Maybe she's going someplace where she feels more at home," he said.

"Is it true what that guard told us?" Chicks asked as they all walked back along the Pike to the Temple of Palmistry. "That there ain't no reward for catching us now?"

Jack nodded. "It's true, all right." But his smile wasn't as glad as it could be, and Frances knew why.

"But, um, speaking of rewards," Frances began. She knew the older boys got along with her the best, so she figured she ought to deliver the bad news. "We found the owner of the medallion. But . . . there wasn't a reward." *Not money, anyway,* she thought to herself.

Finn's face fell. "Oh," he said, putting his hands in his pockets.

Owney shrugged. "I figured."

"That's just how it goes," Dutch mumbled. "Stuff like that, it's always too good to be true."

"The thing is, though," Alexander said suddenly, "we *do* have something we can share with you."

Frances and Jack exchanged confused looks. *What was he talking about?*

Alexander reached into his pocket and pulled out a roll of bills. Right away Frances realized what it was.

Jack did, too. "The steamboat fare!" he whispered. They'd forgotten all about it.

"Mr. Zogby gave this to us," Alexander explained, "so that we could travel first-class on the *Addie Dauphin*. . . ."

The memory came back to Frances. "But the man selling tickets told us to ride with the 'river rats,' and so we kept the fare. Saved it."

Dutch grinned. "River rats. That's us!"

"Anyway," said Alexander, "Mr. Zogby gave that money to us because he wanted us to have a good journey. . . ."

"And we did! Thanks to you," Jack told the older boys.

"You helped us escape!" Eli said.

Alexander looked around at his friends' faces. By now Frances had guessed what Alexander wanted to do, and she nodded, as if to say *Go ahead.* Jack nodded, too.

The older boys guessed, too. "You're sharing that money with us?" Finn said. "After everything that's happened?"

"Like when we took your medallion," Dutch said. "Because we didn't trust you. I mean, we never trust anyone!"

"But do you trust us now?" Alexander asked.

Dutch didn't say anything for a moment or two. He exchanged glances with Finn and Chicks and Owney.

Finally they nodded their heads. *Yes.*

"Let's shake hands!" Dutch said, reaching out with his. When he got to Frances, he bowed. "Was a pleasure meeting you, Queenie."

She laughed. "Likewise, Mr. Dutch."

Owney spoke up. "I know what we should do with the money! The four of us can take a train somewheres. Someplace we can be on our own. And where we can start our *own* Wanderville."

Alexander's face lit up. "That's . . . that's a fine idea! An *amazing* idea!"

"Can there be more than one Wanderville?" Harold asked.

Alexander reached over and tousled his red hair. "Sure," he said. "Why not? It's a town that can go anyplace. Maybe that includes being in more than one place at a time."

They all decided right then that it would be another law of Wanderville: *There can be as many Wandervilles as anyone ever needs.*

MEET ME IN ST. LOUIS, LOUIS

Back at the Temple of Palmistry, Madame Zee had brought them all sweets from the restaurant at the Streets of Cairo exhibit—pieces of Turkish delight, sweet cakes, and little round doughnuts dripping with honey.

All ten of them—Jack and his friends, Eli's cousin, and Dutch's gang—sat on the pillows and carpets in the front room, eating all they could and listening to Madame Zee's stories of fortune-telling and performing illusions.

"In fact," she said. "I will tell my own fortune now. I foretell that my son Philander will read in the newspaper about Mr. Adolphius. And then he will send me a telegram!"

"I think that will happen!" Eli said. "I hope it's soon."

Afterward, Madame Zee gave them all the leftovers wrapped in paper and wrote down her address in Frances's reader so that they could write to her one day.

Then they walked to the end of the Pike to the exit gate, where Dutch, Finn, Chicks, and Owney bade them goodbye. There were train tracks that ran outside the gate, and the older boys said they were going to follow them on foot for a while.

"Maybe we'll find a freight car and ride the rails, like you did," Finn said.

"If you ever come across a couple of kids named Quentin and Lorenzo," Jack told them, "say hello for us." He didn't know if they would ever possibly meet, but he hoped so.

The older boys waved one last time through the gate, and then they were on their way.

The group turned to head toward the grander plazas and palaces of the Exposition where they'd walked the day before. But in front of the great monument, Eli suddenly stopped.

"Speaking of goodbyes . . ." he said.

Jack had a heavy feeling in his chest all of a sudden.

"I've been thinking about family a lot," Eli said. "And then today when Madame Zee was talking about her son, I was thinking about family a lot more. And then . . ." He looked over at his cousin Willie. "I *found* my family! I think maybe it all means something, you know?"

"What's that?" Jack asked, though he was starting to understand what Eli meant.

"Well, being in Wanderville with all of you has made me realize how much I needed to have kinfolk. I never really had that with my pop. But *you* became my kin."

There was a lump in Jack's throat, but it was all right. Harold sniffled a little, but he smiled, too.

"But now," Eli continued, "I have a chance to be with my mama's family. Willie says there's room for me to live with my aunt and uncle, and they're good people." Eli's cousin nodded. "Anyway. Whenever you head out for California, I just wanted to let you know I'm staying here."

Frances reached out and squeezed Eli's hand. "I'm glad you have family."

Jack nodded. "Me, too."

Eli and Willie hung back by the lagoon bridge to talk about plans. Now it was just the four of them, walking along the plaza paths to get one last good look at the World's Fair. They walked quietly for a while, watching the Ferris wheel turn in the distance and listening to the music that floated from some of the palaces. There was a song about the Fair that Jack realized they'd been hearing all along, with a refrain that went:

Meet me in St. Louis, Louis,
Meet me at the Fair
Don't tell me the lights are shining
Anyplace but there . . .

"'Anyplace but there,'" Frances sang softly. "But you know what the marvelous thing is? We're *here*."

"In Wanderville?" Harold asked, looking around at all the palaces. "Is *this* Wanderville right now?"

Jack took everything in—the water cascades, the towers, the terraces. "I think so," he said. "Not just because it all looks like a dream . . ."

"But because we're here together!" Alexander said. "Yes." He turned all around, gazing up at the sky.

Then he stopped turning when he faced Frances and leaned over and kissed her. Right on the mouth!

Harold clapped his hands over his own mouth to muffle a giggle. Jack felt himself grinning, too.

As for Frances, she stepped back and for a moment looked like she might punch Alexander. Then her face turned deep red.

"Give me the map," she said, grabbing it from Alexander's hands. She pretended to study it, a crooked smile on her face. Jack really had to keep himself from laughing out loud then. After a few moments, Frances was sharing the map with Alexander, and her smile had grown bigger.

"Say!" Frances said as she began to look over the map in earnest. "All the states in the union have exhibits here! There's one for Oregon, and South Dakota . . . and one for California!" She put down the map. "What do you think, Jack? Should we go *there*?"

Jack knew what Frances was really asking him.

"And by 'we,'" Alexander said, meeting Jack's eyes, "that means you too, you know. Where do you want to go? Back to New York?"

Jack knew what he wanted to tell them. He'd known, in fact, for a while, but he hadn't been able to say why he felt that way. But now, as he looked up to see the afternoon clouds drift by the palaces—not like a dream at all, he realized, but like Frances said, just *here*—he knew why.

"I want to go where my family is," Jack said at last. "And by 'family' . . ." He took a deep breath. "I mean all of you."

It felt good to say it. All he'd ever wanted was to be there when someone truly needed him. Now he would be there for them.

Harold grinned. "I know."

"Me, too," said Alexander. He reached over and squeezed Frances's hand, and then she kept their hands clasped.

Frances's eyes were bright. "So we're going to California?" she asked. "The real California, I mean?"

Jack laughed. "We're going," he said. "For real."